MW01681096

Belle Publishing LLC Presents…

Belle Publishing LLC

KILLA CITY II
THE EULOGY

For permission requests, write to the publisher, addressed "Attention: Permissions Coordinator," at the address below.

Belle Publishing LLC

Oklahoma City, Ok 73142

www.bellepublishingllc.co

bellepublishingllc@gmail.com

Ordering Information:

Quantity sales. Special discounts are available on quantity purchases by corporations, associations, and others. For details, contact the publisher at the address above

First Edition

ISBN- 978-1-953928-18-4

ACKNOWLEDGEMENT

First off, I wanna thank God for every single blessing he has given me throughout my life. It's been a great run so far. The support from everyone has been amazing.

Speaking of support, I wanna thank my best friend, my side kick, my wife Courtney. The amount of patience you have had with me during this journey has been wonderful and I thank you for being my inspiration.

Anthony Crawford, my brother and friend, has been a day one supporter. From proofreading to editing to giving me the knowledge to push forward. You bless everything you touch and I'm grateful you touched Killa City.

I also wanna thank Sharita Renee for being the most supportive friend I could ask for. You always showed even when no one else did and I thank you.

Poetic City I thank you for the fire you put into Killa City II

My Killa City Squad, you know what it is. Because of you I have truly maximized my existence.

My mother's Ida Mae, Rosie, and Mechie have been my number one fans since my first book released. They will truly keep me writing.

One of the greatest with a camera, Sunee Rice. Her camera took us to another level and I thank you and Sunee Rice Photography.

Finally, I want to thank Belle Publishing. Kenyetta and Courtney seen something in me that I didn't see myself. They took my writing on paper and made it a masterpiece and now you have the Killa City Trilogy. They are nowhere near done so keep your eyes open. Much more to come.

FACEBOOK: Killa City. The Urban Mind of Kinfolks
IG: killacityg
bellepublishingllc.co
bellepublishingllc@gmail.com

Chapter 1

Yetta stepped outside the hospital room before putting the phone back to her ear. She said, "You got balls even calling me after shooting my brother. Have you lost your mind, or have you finally realized how stupid you are?"

Nick laughed. "Damn I miss that fire," he said, trying to get a smile.

"What the fuck you want Nick," she said irritated. "I really don't feel like going down memory lane today."

He hit the blunt before he said, "Yetta, all this anger is unnecessary. What you expect, me to be a worker all my life? Naw Baby, I'm a King and it's time for me to take my Crown."

Yetta laughed aloud. The nurse at the desk walked up and asked her to quiet down and Yetta apologized. "A KING? Boy please, you barely a captain in ya'll little shack. You really think ya nuts big enough to fuck with Gripp? Naw, you already a dead man walking boo."

Nick sat up. "Look bitch, this could've gone nice but as usual, you talk too much. Ya best choice would be to get out of town. Bout to get really bloody in KILLA CITY."

"Nigga do it look like we run from a fight?" She said cutting him off. "Bitch we eat beef for breakfast."

"SHUT THE FUCK UP!" Nick screamed through the phone. "You better act like you know. Think this shit a fucking game? I got heavyweights backing me; killers coming from all angles. I was only giving you a courtesy call cause of our history but if you get hit, then so be it. Gripp and Ma Williams will fall in line."

"BOY STOP. Ain't nobody backing your dumb ass. You think Gripp became the King of KILLA CITY lightly? You think my Ma gonna fall in ya line? Then you truly dumber than I thought." She said laughing.

He paused and then said, "Green, Hassan, and the Baker Brothers." Yetta took a deep breath over the phone as Nick continued, "LEAVE YETTA."

Nick hung up in Yetta's face. She paused and turned to view Tony lying on the hospital bed. She couldn't believe what she had just heard. "Why the fuck would Green and Hassan come together against Gripp? At least now we know who the bank is," she thought to herself. She unlocked her phone and dialed Gripp's number.

"Hey Yetta. What's up?" Gripp said as he answered the phone.

"Hey Gripp," she said while taking a deep breath. "We got a problem."

"What's that?" he asked, hearing the irritation in her voice. "Doctor say something bout Tony?

"Naw, Tony's good," she replied.

"What is it then?" Gripp asked, sitting up in the truck.

"Well, I know who is banking Nick. The fucker just called me."

"Who called you? Nick?" Gripp asked. "What the fuck did he say Yetta?"

Yetta took the phone from her ear and took a deep breath. "NIGGA," she whispered before putting it back to her ear. "This Nigga just talked a bunch of shit and said he is backed by Green and Hassan."

"Wait a Fucking minute. You mean this Nigga Green rolling the fucking dice? He didn't learn from the last time about fucking with me and mine?" Gripp looked at Bee before speaking again. "Is that all he said?"

Yetta took a long pause. "He also said the Baker Brothers."

"Ain't that a Bitch," Gripp said, smiling. "That's how you know I'm the king right there."

"What you mean?" Yetta asked.

"The Baker Brothers don't take contracts on royalty unless it's a seven-figure contract. My life worth at least a million," He responded while laughing.

"Really Gripp? That's what you got from that?" she asked while laughing.

"Honestly, Yetta, I don't give a fuck bout none of them. I'm the King of KILLA CITY, let 'em come. I'm waiting," Gripp said smiling.

Yetta looked up to see Dr. McFadden walking towards the room. "Hey, here goes the doctor, I'll call you back," Yetta said to Gripp.

"Bet," Gripp said, hanging up the phone.

Yetta hung up the phone as she walked back into the room. Dr McFadden came in behind her.

"Hello, Dr. McFadden," Yetta said as she sat down.

"Hello, Yetta," Dr. McFadden said as she picked up Tony's chart.

"So, when can Tony go home?"

"Everything looks good. Vitals, blood pressure, and EKG all normal, so I should be able to send him home tomorrow with meds and a follow up appointment."

Yetta smiled. "Thank you, Dr. McFadden." She got up and walked to the bed. She touched the top of Tony's head. "Is there anyway that info can stay between us?"

Dr. McFadden looked at Yetta for a few seconds. She thought about who she was dealing with. "Sure, I don't think that will be a problem," she said, smiling. She put the chart down. "I will let you know when you guys can leave." She turned and left the room.

Yetta turned and stood by the window as her mind was putting everything together. "Who knew the past would come back this hard. Damn," she thought to herself as she pulled out her phone and texted Bam. "I need a fucking blunt."

Gripp hung up the phone heated. He thought about what Yetta told him. He smiled as he looked at Bee with evil in his eyes.

"Baby? You good?" Bee asked him.

"I'm fucking great baby. Hell, I need some exercise anyway. These frails not bothering my mental I'm just ready to eat."

Bee laughed and said, "All you think about is food."

"That's cause I stay hungry," Gripp said laughing. "After we eat, I want you to take the kids and dip to ya people spot in Tulsa. Shits bout to get real and you know how I am when the war is on."

Bee thought for a second and asked, "So you really are gonna go to war with Nick? Even after finding out he has hired the Baker Brothers?"

"Hell Yeah. Why the fuck would I not?" Gripp asked calmly.

"Baby, you know as well as I do the Bakers don't miss a target and no one ever knows they are coming," she said with concern in her eyes. "I understand you're King but what if…."

Gripp cut her off and said, "Stop that girl. You know better than to think like that. No one takes KILLA CITY. I know bout them niggas but them niggas don't know bout me, my city, or my streets. It is what it is baby."

Bee sat back in her seat. She had been with Gripp long enough to know what his statement meant. "Alright Gripp, do what you gotta do but you better bring your ass home," she said while punching his chest.

"I got you," he responded, pulling her closer in his arms. He kissed her with passion so hard her toes curled. "I'm ready to eat," he concluded with that look on his face.

Bee smiled, because she knew what that meant.

"Stop Gripp," she said playfully. "Wait till we get home."

Gripp laughed, "Aight. Yo turn up the music."

The driver did as he drove to the restaurant.

HASSAN
Rest in Love
9/30/91-5/22/19

CHAPTER 2

Nick was rolling a blunt when he heard a knock on his door. "Who the fuck is that this time of night?" He asked himself. He finished rolling and grabbed his Glock. He walked to the door and looked through the peephole. He opened the door and took a step back so Green and Hassan could walk in.

"What the fuck are ya'll doing at my crib?" Nick asked putting the strap in his waist. "You know good and fucking well we not supposed to be seen together."

Green held up his hand. "That's the problem, you think you're in control when you're not." Green put his hand down and sat on the couch. "Now I chose you because I thought you would get the job done, but now I'm having doubts. Why is Gripp still standing? Why does Ma Williams still have control of states that are supposed to belong to me? Should I just kill you instead?"
Hassan pulled out his gun and slid the chamber back.

Nick looked at him and laughed. "Nigga please," he said sitting down. "Ya bitch ass chose me because your ass too scared to go up against Ma Williams after Gripp hurt ya team the last time. And Hassan, you ain't got the nuts to pull that trigger. You just an errand boy."

"Bitch ass nigga!" Hassan yelled as he walked up and put the gun in Nick's face. Nick laughed and lit his blunt.

"That's enough Hassan," Green said.

Hassan gave him a long look before putting down the gun.

Nick laughed and said, "Like I said, errand boy. Ya'll done cause I got better shit to do?"

"Yeah, we done," Green answered while getting up. "But I better hear something from you soon." They walked to the door.

"You just concentrate on the product old man, leave the streets to us Thugs."

Green turned and gave Nick a look of despair.

"Soon Nick. Or we will make other moves," Green responded as they walked out the door.

Nick closed the door and proudly said, "Whatever. I'm gonna kill them anyway." He went to the bedroom and laid down.

"TEGOOOO," Pain enthusiastically said as he and Big Rick got out the car. "What's good with ya Cuz?"

"Shit MAINTAINING Folks!" Tego answered as they shook hands. "What's good with you? What's up Big Rick?"

"Shit, Love One! How that insane life, G?" Big Rick asked showing Tego love.

"Could be better," Tego answered. "Ya'll come on in." Big Rick and Pain walked into the house. "What ya'll doing here anyway?" Tego asked as he closed the door. "Ma Williams shut down the pipeline."

"Now Tego, you know those rules don't apply to Gripp. And why does it smell like blood in ya crib?" Pain looked around the room. "What happen Cuz?"

"Man, when Ma sent word, Texas had just pulled into town," Tego answered while shaking his head. "They didn't think the rules applied to them either, so Blow blasted 'em."

"What?" Pain said shocked, looking at Blow. "Why the fuck you kill em? This is neutral grounds Cuz and doing stupid shit like that will fuck up more than this spot. What were you thinking?"

"Nigga, I was thinking I'm going home to my kids and not to Vance Funeral home," Blow responded, still sweeping the floor. "Neutral or not nobody comes to CRIME BLUFF and disrespect Ma Williams. I took the bodies to Dixon Road, so it looks like a Little Rock murder so we good."

Pain thought about it, Blow was on point. "My bad, Blow, good looking out."

"Already, now take ya ass over there and roll a blunt," Blow said laughing. "I'm gonna get ya'll ready."

"Bet!" Pain said picking up the tray. As he broke down the weed, his phone rang. He looked and seen it was Bam. He swiped to answer, "What up Bam?"

"Ba, Ba, Ba" was all Pain could hear.

"Bam?" Pain yelled as the phone hung up. He looked at his phone, confused. "What the fuck was that about?" He was about to call Bam back when Blow came out the back. He put down his phone and went to check the work.

KESHA AND DOE

CHAPTER 3

Bam was at the house getting Tony's clothes before he went to pick him and Yetta up from the hospital. After packing a bag and taking two shots of D'usse, he headed to the garage. He got in Gripp's Mustang and started it up.

He pulled out his phone and called Yetta. She answered on the second ring. "Hey baby. I'm bout to leave Tony's. Do you need anything before I get there?"

"Hey Daddy, I'm good just make sure you bring a blunt."

"I got you baby. I love you. See ya'll in a few."

"I love you too," she said smiling. "See you soon."

He hung up the phone, hit the garage button and put the car in reverse. As he was backing out, something hit the car. He put the car in park and got out to see what it was. When he stepped out the car, a bullet hit his leg. He screamed as he fell to the ground. He pulled out his gun and looked around but didn't see anyone. Hc pulled out his phone and dialed Pain's number. While the phone was ringing, another shot rang out, hitting him in the chest. He flew back. The phone fell by his ear.

Marcus and Tim walked up and stood over Bam. They could hear him wailing, "Ba Ba Ba." Tim reached down and picked up his phone. "Pain, huh?" He pressed end.

"Yo Tim, this ain't that nigga, Gripp, bro. Who the fuck is this?"

"Fuck bruh! I don't know," Tim answered confusedly. "I do know this is Gripp's whip. Fuck I hate killing extra people. Who the fuck are you?" Tim asked Bam. "Yo, call Shirley."

Bam held up his hand and gave Tim the finger. Marcus laughed as he pulled out his phone. He had a text from Shirley, saying that Bam was a part of the contract. "Kill him," Marcus demanded as he walked off. Tim shot Bam two more times then spat on his lifeless body. He turned to follow Marcus. They both got in a SUV and drove off.

"So, what now, Tim? That's the only lead we had on this nigga. How the fuck we gonna find him now?"

"Chill bruh. I got a plan. We gonna make him come to us. Let's go to the room so I can figure this shit out," Tim concluded while pulling out his phone. "Plus, it's my Facebook time."

"So, you not gonna hit Nick?" Marcus asked.

"Naw. What's the point? Gripp still walking and he ain't paying extra. Just no more freebies," Tim said, looking at his timeline.

"Whatever," Marcus said turning up the music and driving to the hotel.

Kesha woke up from her nap and noticed she was still at her dad's house. She stretched and got out the bed. She walked to the bathroom and stood looking at herself in the mirror.

"Damn, look at me. All this crying got my eyes puffy," she said while wetting a towel and cleaning her face. She walked out the bathroom, got clothes from her closet, and then went to shower. She washed her body slow as the water hit her soft skin, masking the tears falling from her eyes.

She turned off the water and stepped out the shower. She sat on the bed and put on lotion before getting dressed. She walked downstairs and seen Doe sitting in the kitchen eating watermelon.

"Hey Doe! Seriously?" She inquired while laughing and looking at the plate.

"Hey Kesha!" Doe said pulling his head from the watermelon. "You know I need my energy! How you doing?"

"I'm ok. Ready to take my baby home. What time they supposed to be leaving the hospital?"

"I don't know," Doe answered, looking at his watch. "I will call Yetta and find out."

"OK," Kesha said, walking to the fridge. "I'm gonna grab a sandwich."

"Bet!" Doe said, pulling out his phone to call Yetta.

Yetta answered the phone after a few rings, "Hey Doe! What's up?"

"Not Shit. Wondering what time ya'll getting out of there?"

Yetta looked at her watch and worriedly replied, "Bam called and said he was leaving Tony's house a couple of hours ago. He should have been here."

"Oh, yeah?" Doe inquisitively said. "That ain't even like Bam. Have you tried to call him?"

"Honestly naw. I've been laughing at Dr. McFadden trying to convince Tony he needs bed rest. That nigga ain't trying to hear shit, act like he didn't just get shot in the chest," she said laughing.

Doe laughed, "Yeah, that sound like Tony."

"For real!"

"Aight, so Bam never made it with Tony clothes?"

"Naw he didn't!"

Doe thought for a second and spoke to Kesha, "Aye Kesha, call Bam real quick ma."

"OK," Kesha said concerned while dialing Bam's number. When the voicemail came on, she sat her phone down and looked at Doe. "He didn't answer."

"What the Fuck!" Doe angrily said, getting tight. "Aight Yetta, me and Kesha gonna slide by Tony's spot and grab some things; then we will head that way. Call me if you hear from Bam."

"Alright bet. See ya'll in a minute."

"YADADI," Doe said hanging up. "Yo Kesha, grab ya shit and let's go."

Doe got up, walked out the living room, and went to Gripp's gun safe. He grabbed two foldaway nine's and closed the safe. Kesha was at the door when he came out.

"Uh Doe?" she asked, looking at the guns. "Is there a problem?"

"I don't know, Kesha," he answered, handing her one of the guns, "But I do know Bam ain't that Nigga. My trigger finger itching."

"Bam ass probably fell asleep at my house," Kesha rebutted, putting the gun in her purse. "You know that nigga barely sleeps."

"Kesha, this is one time I hope you're right," Doe expressed while opening the door.

They walked outside. Doe unlocked the minivan. Kesha looked at him crazy.

"Why the fuck are we driving the maids minivan Doe?" she asked. "I'm not getting in that shit." Doe laughed,

"Kesha, we at war and the last thing them pussy ass niggas looking for is Goons in a minivan." Kesha looked at Doe. He thumped her nose and they both laughed then got in the van. Doe lit a blunt and gave it to Kesha. “It ain’t that bad,” he said, smiling. He drove away, headed towards Tony and Kesha’s crib.

Kesha pulled out her phone and called Pain as she hit the blunt. When he answered, she turned down the radio.

“What’s good sis? Everything OK?” Pain asked.

“Hopefully. Have you heard from Bam?”

“Not since he called me this morning playing on the phone. Breathing hard and shit. Might have been sleep.”

“What? What time was that Bro?” She asked while pondering.

"Shit, bout 8:30 this morning!" Pain replied, looking at his call log. "Why you asking all these questions? Did something happen to my nigga?"

"Naw," Kesha said. "We just haven't heard from him since and he was supposed to pick up Tony and Yetta from the hospital hours ago; and he not answering his phone."

"That nigga probably sleep," Pain said laughing. "He will pop up sooner or later."

"Yeah? We on our way to the house to grab some clothes."

"Who you with?"

"I'm with Doe."

"I can dig it! Hit me after ya'll get Tony."

"OK. What the hell you doing anyway? You back in *KILLA CITY* yet?"

"Naw, I'm still in *CRIME BLUFF* fucking with Tego ass."

"OK I will call you later. Be careful."

"Already sis. Gone." They both hung up.

"So, Pain said he hasn't heard from him since this morning. He said that he sounded like he was sleep," Kesha said looking at Doe.

"What you mean he sounded like he was sleep?" Doe said, tight.

"Breathing in the phone." Doe drove faster once she said that. "What is it Doe?" she asked grabbing her seatbelt.

“I have known Bam for fifteen years and one thing I know is he don’t sleep by his phone. Somethings up.”

“Fuck!” Kesha yelled, sitting back.

When they were a block away, Doe stopped the Van.

“Lock and load Kesha. Just in case.” He handed her a clip. They both popped the nine’s and put in the clips. Doe slowly drove to the house.

“DOE STOP!” Kesha screamed when she seen Gripp’s car in front of the garage. “Why the fuck is my dad’s car out?” They got out and started walking with guns drawn. Doe noticed the drivers door open. He looked at Kesha and they both went towards the car. As Doe moved right, Kesha moved left.

When they were behind the car, Kesha saw blood behind the tires. When she looked around the car, she instantly dropped her gun and started screaming,

“NOOOOOOOO! Bam get up! No, no, no! Get up!” She reached down and put Bam’s head on her lap as Doe came around the car.

He stopped in his tracks when he seen his homie laid out on the ground and angrily yelled “SON OF A BITCH! HOW THE FUCK THEY GET MY NIGGA? AND HERE OF ALL PLACES? FUCK FUCK FUCK!” Doe put his gun back up and went to check the rest of the house. He came back and sat beside Kesha, seeing the tears fall from her eyes.

"Why Doe?" she asked sobbing. "How am I gonna tell Yetta this shit. Oh Bam!" She kept rubbing his head. Bam had been like a brother to her most of her life. He had been Pain's ace since day one.

Doe was speechless. He got up, looked at Kesha, and said,

"Kesha, ya'll still got them cameras here?" He picked up his gun.

Kesha kissed Bam on the head and laid him back down. She got up and looked at Doe. "Fucking right come on!" she answered as they walked in the house. Doe pulled out his phone and called White.

"Detective White," White answered cheerfully.

"Yo, send an ambulance to Tony crib. No cops!"

"Tony's?" White responded confusedly. "What's going on that way?"

"Nigga do what the fuck you told and stop asking questions," Doe said before he hung up in White's face. "Fucking Dumbass." Kesha went to the room and pulled up the video. Doe was standing beside her. "Right there Kesha!" She played the tape and they saw Bam backing out of the garage. They watched as he fell, tried to call someone, and hit the ground. When the two men walked up to Bam, Doe paused it.

"You got to be fucking kidding me," Doe said while staring at Marcus Baker's face on the screen. "The Baker Brothers? Why the fuck would they kill Bam."

Kesha looked surprised and asked, "Who the fuck are the Baker Brothers? And where should I send that black dress?" She stood up.

"Naw Kesha. The Bakers are hired guns and not cheap and everyone who went at them has missed thus far. The only ones that came close are Big Rick and Blake. But now, we on that ass. They killed the wrong nigga today."

Kesha looked up and saw the ambulance pull into the driveway with Detective White following. Kesha and Doe both walked outside. White parked and got out of his truck.

"Doe, Kesha, now what is going on?" White asked.

Doe looked at him and responded, "You bout a hard-headed bitch. Somebody killed Bam. He is over there by Gripp's car."

White stood still. He motioned for the paramedics to get Bam. "Let's go watch the video and see what exactly happened here," he said looking at the front door.

"Ain't no video," Doe said. "Me and Kesha already looked."

White got irritated and replied, "Well I will call Gripp and let…."

Doe interjects, "You won't do shit but make sure Bam gets to the morgue. Get in ya car and do ya job." Doe pushed him towards the car.

Kesha went inside and grabbed some clothes for her and Tony. When she came back out, she could see Doe pushing White. She walked over and grabbed Doe by the arm. "Let's go Doe," she demanded as they turned and got back in the van.

Doe sat back and watched as they put Bam in the ambulance. He looked at his phone for a moment and said, "Kesha, I gotta call Gripp."

She just shook her head then sat back in the seat. Doe dialed Gripp's number.

"Doe, my Nigga. What's good?" Gripp answered.

"Yo, shits bad Boss, mean bad-bad."

"Fuck! What now?" Gripp asked as he noticed that Doe got quiet and he could hear someone crying in the background. "Doe? Who in the car with you? What the fuck happened?"

Doe took a deep breath, "That's Kesha Cuz. Assholes got Bam Boss."

Gripp stood up and walked to the other side of the room. "WHAT THE FUCK YOU MEAN THEY GOT BAM? WHO?" Gripp said angrily.

"He was supposed to pick up clothes for Tony," Kesha said. "And they got him at the house driving your car. He had been dead for a minute before we got there."

Gripp punched a wall. All types of anger flowed through his body. "SO, WHO THE FUCK PULLED THE TRIGGER?"

"The Baker Brothers. Me and Kesha watched the video. And I want Blood," Doe answered.

"Bakers, huh? Ok, meet me at Ma Williams' hotel. It's time to get bloody," Gripp exclaimed as he hung up the phone and sat in his chair. “Fucking Bam, rest easy nigga. And don’t worry, I will kill them myself.” He got up and went downstairs.

KEISHA

CHAPTER 4

Kesha tried to wipe her face before they walked in the hospital room but as soon as Tony seen her, he knew.

"Baby, what is it? Why you got them tears in your eyes like I'm not going home?" Tony asked while smiling.

Kesha didn't say anything. She just walked over to the bed and put herself in Tony's arms with tears still falling down her face. Tony looked at Doe.

"Yo, what is it?" He asked as Yetta walked back in with his ice water.

"Hey" Yetta interjects. "I'm so glad to see ya'll cause I'm so ready to go. Bam ass gonna hear about this shit," she said joking.

Kesha sobbed louder when Yetta said that. Tony looked up at Doe then at Yetta. Doe didn't say a word.

"Yo what the fuck happened?" Tony asked while pulling himself up. "What happened? Where's Bam?"

"He's downstairs baby," she said sobbing.

"Downstairs? Where's the car? Well, shit let's go," Tony said reaching for his shirt.

"Tony," Yetta said. Tony turned and looked at his sister. He then realized by the look on her face where Bam was. He looked at Doe.

"How they get him FOLKS?" Tony asked with anger filling his body.

"This morning leaving ya crib," Doe responded, rubbing his head.

"At my crib? Who the fuck was it?" Tony stood up.

"Bakers, the hit men," Doe responded.

"Bakers?" Tony instantly said. "How the fuck they know where my house is? Only the crew knows that."

Doe thought for a second. Tony had a good point. "Bruh I don't know but we will find out."

Kesha got up and grabbed Yetta and pulled her tight. She tried not to scream but it just came out.

"AHHHHH. Why the fuck did this shit happen?" She screamed with tears falling from her eyes. "I wanna see him Kesha."

Kesha looked at Yetta. She knew, if the shoe was switched, she would want the same.

"OK. Let's go. We'll be back." They left the room headed to the morgue.

"Yo, Doe!" Tony said when they left. "What's the plan? Where the fuck these nigga's at?"

"Naw bruh, your plan is bed rest," Doe said, pushing him back on the bed, we got this."

"Fuck you mean?" Tony asked, heated. "I ain't bed resting shit. Niggas came to my house which means they know more than we think. If ya'll go without me I'm calling Black."

Doe laughed. Martelle, also known as Black, was the funniest killer alive. He was always killing people in funny ways. It was entertainment at its best.

"Bruh, Black retired. His ass not leaving Hot Springs for nothing."

"Man, that's my nigga. If I call, he gonna come," Tony said getting dressed. Everyone has a price Doe, you know that."

"Righteous," Doe said while handing Tony his Jordan's. "Come on. Let's go meet the girls and get out this damn place." As they walked out the room, they ran into Dr. McFadden.

"Tony," she said. "I see you're going home. I'm sorry about Larondon. I seen Kesha and Yetta on the elevator."

"Thanks Doc," Tony said. "And thank you for taking care of this fine body."

Dr. McFadden smiled, "Take care of yourself."

"I'll do my best," Tony said. She gave him his discharged paperwork and they walked to the elevator. Once they were in and the doors closed, Doe looked at Tony and asked, "Yo, you wanna see Bam?"

"Naw," Tony responded. "I wanna see the niggas that killed him."

The elevator stopped on the first floor. They met Kesha and Yetta as they were walking towards the exit.

Doe looked at the ladies and saw the exhaustion on their faces.

"Yo, I'm gonna take ya'll to Gripp spot. We all could use some rest," Doe said as he picked up his phone and sent Gripp a text. After getting in the van, they drove towards Nichols Hills.

Tony asked Yetta for his phone. When she gave it to him, he dialed Yella's number. He answered on the second ring.

"Tony G. What's good with ya Bruh. Feeling better?" Yella asked, happy to hear his homie's voice.

"Yeah bruh, I'm feeling ok, but we got major problems."

"There go that word again," Yella said, shaking his head. "I'm bout tired of problems. What's the deal now?"

"The Baker Brothers killed Bam this morning at my house."

Yella got quiet.

"Damn, how in the fuck is that possible? Who talking?" Yella and Tony had the same mindset.

"I don't know bruh but it's some shit going on. We on our way to Gripp spot for the night."

"Cool," Yella said. "I'll meet ya'll there."

"Bet. Gone," Tony said as they hung up.

.

Gripp was getting ready to go see Ma Williams when his phone went off. He read the text from Doe and sat the phone back down. When he turned, the phone started ringing. He looked and seen it was Ma Williams calling. He swiped to answer,

"Hello, Ma Williams," He said when he answered. "I was just about to head your way."

"No need. I heard about Bam getting shot at my son's house, in your car. Is that what you were coming to tell me?"

"Part of it but there is more," Gripp said, sitting on the couch.

"There is Gripp; much more. More like a million-dollar contract on your head?"

Gripp smiled because he loved that type of shit.

He said, "Ma Williams, I'm not worried bout Nick or the Baker Brothers, I got better things to think about."

"Really? If you had been in that car it would be you dead instead of Bam. Has that crossed your mind?"

"It has among other things but for that to happen someone had to talk."

"What makes you think that?"

"Because Tony works for me, but he is your son and you put those houses in places only certain people could find which makes his house the safe spot. The question is how did the Baker Brothers find it?"

Ma Williams thought for a second. She continued,

"Good question Gripp. Have everyone at the church in the morning. After service, I will meet with your crew before I fly back to Crime Bluff."

"I got you. Have a good night!" he said hanging up. He took a shot of D'usse and dialed Pain's number.

"What's good Gripp," Pain said when he answered the phone. "We was just about to hop on the highway, headed home."

"What's up son!" Gripp said. "I got some news you need to hear."

"Ookaay," Pain said worriedly. "What's the deal?"

"Bam got killed this morning at Tony's. It was the Bakers."

Pain squeezed the phone tight. He looked at Big Rick and told him,

"Head towards Conway." Then he told Gripp, "I will call you back, Pops." Pain hung up the phone. "I'm killing this nigga today." Pain loaded his gun.

"What's the deal folk?" Big Rick asked. "Why we going to Conway?"

"Because Bruh," Pain answered as he mentally plotted. "That's Nick's territory. Time to make the nigga come find me. And when I see either one of the Bakers they ass is mine too."

"Bakers? You talking bout Marcus and Tim?"

"Yeah, you know em?"

"Fuck yeah, that nigga Green hired them to take out Ma Williams a few years back. Me and Blake rocked they ass, but they got away. Then we went and killed Green whole squad. I thought them niggas retired?"

"Apparently not because they killed Bam! My right hand. So, it's on."

"Already!" Big Rick said, exiting the highway.

When they made it to Conway, it was after ten o'clock. Big Rick found a hotel across from IHOP. Pain's phone went off as they were walking in. It was a text from Gripp about church in the morning.

"Guess I'm gonna be late for that," Pain said aloud putting his phone back in his pocket. Go by Smooth the Dude's bar before you go the hotel. I need a drink."

"Bet," Big Rick said as he passed the high school. He turned into the parking lot. "Yo, hand me a Fold-A-Way."

Pain reached in the back and grabbed two Glock nines. He handed one to Big Rick. They got out the car and walked towards the bar.

"You good?" Big Rick asked.

Pain looked at him in despair. Big Rick could see the devil in his eyes as Pain replied,

"I'm Gucci." They went inside the bar.

They sat at a table in the back. Big Rick leaned back so he could watch the door. The waitress came over and they ordered drinks.

"Say, is the owner here tonight?" Pain asked the waitress.

"No, he isn't, but he may slide in before we close," she answered, smiling at Pain.

She left to get their drinks. When she came back, Pain slipped her a bill. She smiled and walked off as the door to the bar opened.

"AHHHHH Shit!" Big Rick said, putting his hand in his pocket. "Look my nigga." He pointed to the door.

Pain turned to see Rasta, Unruly, and Nell walk inside the bar. They were Nick's top crew in Conway.

Pain smiled. He looked at Big Rick as he pulled out his nine and folded it out. He watched as the trio went to a table and sat down. The same waitress went to take their drink orders. Nell started yelling at the waitress then slapped her pad out of her hand. As she went to pick it up, Unruly poured the basket of chips on her head. She got up and ran to the back as they laughed loudly inside the bar.

Pain got up and walked to their table."What's good?" He said. "Why you gotta treat this lady like that? You lost ya fucking mind or something?"

Nell stood up and said, "Now who the fuck is you." Before he could finish his words, Pain slapped him so hard, his body did a three sixty.

Unruly jumped up and Pain backed away, watching him. Unruly angrily asked, "Nigga do you know who the fuck we are?" He reached for his gun.

"Nigga, don't you got a kid to take care of?" Pain asked while laughing. "All this money and ya ass behind on child support and got the nerve to treat a woman like that? Bitch Please."

"Nigga you don't know me!" Unruly said, pointing his gun at Pain. "Who the fuck are you?"

"I'm that nigga and I don't have to know you," Pain said. "I know the streets and they talk bout your raggedy ass everywhere."

"Dude you got me fucked up. Your mouth bout to get you in some shit playboy."

"Playboy?" Pain questioned while shaking his head. "See that's the shit I'm talking about you fucking frail. Matter of fact, ain't it your day to take a bath you nasty little boy."

Unruly went to grab Pain but Big Rick moved fast. He reached and grabbed Unruly by his dreads and pulled him from the table. Rasta pulled her gun and got off a shot but missed. Pain knocked the gun out of her hand then slammed her head on the table.

"Who the fuck am I itty bitty ass nigga?" Pain asked angrily. "Bitch I'm Pain Loc from *KILLA CITY.*" Pain raised his leg and kicked Rasta in the knee breaking her stance. He then grabbed her and Nell by their dreads and walked out the bar dragging them behind. By the time he made it outside, some of Nell's dreads came out. "Nappy Bitch," Pain said, throwing the hair on the ground. He pulled out his gun and pointed it at Unruly. "Where the fuck is Nick?" Unruly didn't answer fast enough for Pain. "Yo, Big Rick, shoot that bitch."

Big Rick pulled out his gun and shot Rasta in the chest.

"Now, you got about ten minutes before this bitch bleed to death so let's try this again. Where's Nick?" Pain asked, looking at Nell.

"Nigga do you know who Mama is?" Nell asked while looking scared. "You must not know who you fucking with?"

"You know I don't know who I'm fucking with," Pain said looking around, but neither did ya'll when you stepped to *KILLA CITY*. Now I'm not gonna ask again."

"*KILLA CITY?*" Nell cluelessly said. "I'm the seed of FeFe, ain't nobody worried bout *KILLA CITY*. Nick gonna kill you niggas anyway."

Unruly laughed and spit on Pain's shoes. Pain punched him in his face so hard he broke his nose.

"Spit now nigga!" Pain said as he continued punching Unruly until Big Rick grabbed his shoulder.

"That nigga dead Folks," Big Rick said, viewing Unrulys's lifeless body.

Pain turned, looked at Nell, and concluded, "And so you know, I'm the seed of Gripp, bitch." Pain pulled the trigger and watched as Nell's body hit the ground. He looked at Big Rick and said, "Let's ride bruh." They got in the car and drove off with the music blasting.

Big Rick turned down the music and said, "Yo, that name FeFe sounds familiar, bruh."

"I bet it do. That's ya boy Green's wife. Married him right before ya'll ran them off."

"Hell Yeah! That's when we went up against the Baker Brothers. Niggas almost had our ass but that nigga Blake too quick for em."

"I can dig it Cuz; either way I just killed her son, so if I can get Green and Nick at the same time. It's done."

"Bet! I'm gonna hit Ma Williams and let her know what's up before church in the morning."

"That's a bet. Yo, what's that on your shirt?" Pain asked, pointing.

Big Rick laughed hard and answered, "That's the nigga Unruly Marcus hair. Nigga take care of his dreads bout like he takes care of his kids. Fucking shame."

They both laughed hard as Pain rolled the blunt.

The next morning Pain stepped outside the room and called Gripp.

"Yeah?" Gripp said when he answered. "You getting ready for church?"

"Naw," Pain said. "I'm in Conway, not gonna make it this morning."

"What? I thought you were coming back last night?"

"MY nigga got killed and I want blood. I went to Smooth Da Dude bar last night and ran into one of Nick's crews."

"Oh yeah," Gripp said, sitting up in the chair. "What the fuck happened?"

"Shit long story short we killed em; one of the niggas was FeFe's son. You know Green's chick?"

"You shitting me, right? Boy you always doing some shit." Gripp began laughing extra hard.

"What's up Gripp?" Pain asked. "You good?"

"Fuck yeah I'm good!" Gripp said, catching his breath. "Green is the nigga bank rolling Nick. Guess now we know why he wants me and Ma Williams dead."

"Yeah, that ain't gonna happen."

"I know, but it's still funny, so when ya'll leaving out?"

"Here in a few," Pain answered. "We gonna stop and gas up then hit the slab."

"Aight, see ya'll later and watch ya backs."

"Already boss. Gone," Pain said as they hung up. He walked back in his room. Big Rick knocked on the door a few minutes later.

"What's good my guy?" Pain asked while showing love.

"Maintaining," Big Rick answered. "About to make this call to Ma Williams. You bout ready to hit the slab?"

"Here in a minute, let me finish packing."

"Cool," Big Rick said dialing Ma Williams. She answered quickly.

"Big Rick!" Ma Williams said quickly. "What the hell is going on in Arkansas? Ya'll shot up a bar last night?"

"No ma'am we shot outside the bar and only hit what was intended to be hit. The niggas killed Pain right hand, Ma Williams, do you think he gonna let that shit ride? Will you?"

"Now you know better than to ask me a question like that, but remember you work for me, not *KILLA CITY.*"

"But we all have a common interest in this, Green is involved, and Pain killed FeFe son last night."

"Yes, Gripp told me about Green sponsoring this adventure. So, what about Nick?"

"Naw just Dude Rasta and Unruly, Big Rick answered. We gonna head back here shortly.

"No," Ma Williams commanded. "I want you and Pain to head towards Little Rock. I'm gonna have Gripp send Yella, Doug D, and Skanes that way as well. It's bout time Gripp show his face."

"What about the Baker Brothers? You gonna put Gripp on front street for them to take out? What kind of plan is this?"

"A great one," Ma Williams answered. "See, while they are looking for Gripp, you, Blake and Pain will be looking for them. By them killing Bam, they think Gripp is here."

"I see ya Ma Williams, but with us killing Dude last night, don't you think Green and FeFe gonna try and make a move?"

"They can try, Gripp got other things in motion as well. This was mostly his idea."

"You giving him control of the situation?"

"I don't have to give him control Big Rick, he already has it. I have told you I'm getting old, and I got faith in Gripp."

"Already, I was wondering who it was gonna be. Guess now I know."

"Gone now, boy, Mama gotta get ready for church," she laughed as she hung up the phone.

Big Rick looked at Pain and, as he sat on the couch, he said, "Guess we don't have to rush bruh."

"What you mean?" Pain asked, putting down his bag. "I just told Gripp we was bout to hit the slab. What we waiting on?"

"Ma Williams sending us to Little Rock."

"Little Rock?" Pain asked confusedly. "What the fuck for?"

"I think I will let Gripp explain that to you when they get there," Big Rick said smiling.

"Oh yeah?" Pain said rubbing his hands together. "It's murder time baby." He grabbed his bags and headed out the door. He turned to look at Big Rick. "You coming Nigga?"

"This Nigga tripping," Big Rick said, getting up and walking out the door.

They hopped in the car and headed for the highway. Big Rick pulled over at the gas station to fill up.

While in the store Pain made some coffee while Big Rick grabbed Red Bulls. They had their backs turned when the first shot flew between them and the register. Pain turned and instantly pulled out his .357 and let it sing. Big Rick jumped behind the counter and came up blasting towards the door. They both stopped shooting and, for a second, it was quiet.

"Come the fuck out" A female screamed. "Ain't no getting away."

"What the fuck?" Big Rick yelled. "Who the fuck are you and why the fuck you popping?"

Right then, they heard shots fired again. "Yo Pain, Big Rick? I got ya'll. Come on out!" Another female voice yelled. Big Rick stood and seen sexy ass Janae standing over two dead bodies. "It's good folks, come on out."

Pain came from behind the chip rack, eating a bag of Munchies.

"Damn," he said looking at Janae like she was a chip in the bag. "Where the hell you come from and who the fuck are they?" He said pointing at the dead bodies.

"Hell, I don't know," Janae replied.

"That's Lil' D and Chicken George," the cashier said, getting up off the floor. "They're security for Green."

Big Rick looked at the cashier then at Pain and said,

"Guess they looking for us." He handed the cashier fifty and started walking out the store.

"What's this for?" The cashier asked while holding the money.

"My gas on pump four," Big Rick responded as he walked out the door.

Pain and Janae followed. When they got outside, it was a truck parked behind their car. Pain instantly pulled his gun.

"Whoa, John Wayne!" Janae said laughing. "That's our ride."

"Oh shit," Pain said, putting his gun away. "Better speak up next time. So, who you got in the truck?"

"I'll introduce you," she answered while motioning the truck to come forward. April and Corey stepped out the truck.

"Yo!" Janae shouted. "This is Big Rick and Pain from *KILLA CITY.* Ya'll, this is April and Corey from Crime Bluff."

"Already," Big Rick said as he pumped gas. "How ya'll know where we was?"

"Gripp called this morning and told us to come watch ya back till he gets here," Janae said. "Lucky I was thirsty and made Corey stop."

"Preciate it," Pain said as he shook Corey's hand.

"Ummhmm," Corey said, getting back in the truck. "Ya'll need to hurry up cause I hate this dry county."

Big Rick laughed as he hung up the nozzle and demanded,

"Yo, Pain, let's ride." They all hopped in their rides and headed to the highway.

Killa City
lla City

CHAPTER 5

After Sunday service, everyone went to Brimmo's Diner. The owner already had a room set up for them to eat. After Gripp talked to the owner, he stepped out as he closed the door. He sat down next to Ma Williams and Bee. Kesha and Yetta both sat at the end of the table. Doug D, Skanes, and Yella sat in the middle while Nine Milli stood by the door. Blake stood behind Ma Williams.

"I hope ya'll enjoyed the service," Ma Williams said speaking to the group. Everyone nodded. "Well you all are here because war has been declared. For those who don't know, we lost Bam yesterday." She looked at Yetta. "I'm so sorry this happened to you baby." Yetta waved her hand but didn't say a word. Ma Williams continued, "Trust me I know you want blood, but we have to get things ready to send him home peacefully."

"So, which one of you the rat?" Yella asked. "The only people that know where that house at are in this room minus three people; and Pain and Big Rick in Arkansas." He looked at Skanes.

Skanes stood up quick and angrily asked, "What the fuck you looking at me for Yella? You know I owe Gripp my life. What the fuck I got to gain?" Skanes crossed his arms.

"Nothing," Yella calmly said. "But ya Bitch do. Tell me, where's Deanna?"

"What the fuck you say?" Skanes asked, leaning on the table.

"What you mean," Yella said, standing up. "You didn't think we would find out bout her bruh?"

"Find out what?" Skanes asked, uncrossing his arms.

"That she is Green's daughter." Yella said. "That she been meeting with Hassan for the last week?" Skanes looked stunned. "See what happens when you don't pay attention to your surroundings." Yella looked around the room and concluded, "Shit gets nasty."

Skanes fell back in his seat as Kesha got up and walked over to him.

"Fam, where that bitch at?" Kesha asked, pulling out her knife. "I mean I would hate to think you involved with this shit." She ran the knife lightly across his hand.

"Yo Kesha, I don't know what…" Kesha put her finger to his lips.

"That don't sound like the answer I wanna hear," She said pushing the knife down on his hand.

"KESHA!" Gripp yelled from the head of the table.

"WHAT?" She snapped at Gripp. She looked at him and pressed harder while Skanes yelled in pain.

Gripp got up from his seat and started to walk towards Kesha, but Yetta made it to her first. She touched the top of Kesha's hand.

"Naw sis. Not here. Not this way," Yetta said, calming Kesha.

Kesha put the knife on the table and walked back to her seat. Yetta took a napkin and handed it to Skanes. He took it and tied it around his hand. Yetta touched his shoulder. When he looked up, he didn't like the look she had on her face. "Bring that bitch to me," Yetta said in a harsh voice. "I'm only gonna say it once." She turned and went to sit next to Kesha.

Gripp looked at the girls then back at Ma Williams. He shook his head then went back to his seat.

"Now listen," Gripp said. "Our beef is not with each other. Skanes, I don't know what the fuck your bitch got to do with this, but like Yetta said she need to see her."

"Understood," Skanes agreed.

"The rest of us will head to Little Rock. We leave at four." Gripp said looking at his watch.

Ma Williams stood up and said, "Kesha, you and Yetta will stay with me so that we can make arrangements for this funeral." She turned and started walking towards the door. Kesha and Yetta got up to follow her out. Before she made it out the door she turned and looked at Gripp.

"You are the King of *KILLA CITY,* and I trust you will handle this accordingly."

"No doubt," Gripp accepted. "Let's get hyphy." Everyone laughed as they got up from the table. They all showed love as they were leaving the diner.

"Remember, four o'clock!" Gripp yelled before getting in his truck.

They all nodded and got in their rides.

Kesha was still heated as they rode in the limo headed to Vance's Funeral Service.

"Kesha," Yetta said, pulling her from her thoughts. "You gonna call and check on Tony before we go in here?"

Kesha looked up to see they had already made it to the funeral home.

"Yes," she said pulling out her phone. "Let me do that now."

"OK," Yetta said, opening the door. "Come on, Ma." Yetta and Ma Williams got out the limo and waited by the door while Kesha made her call.

"What's up Baby?" Tony said when he answered the phone.

"Hey Daddy. How are you feeling?" she asked in a soft voice.

"I'm good," Tony said, sitting up. "Just chilling, smoking on this loud Half Ton brought me. How are you doing? How's my sister?"

"We good, at the funeral home about to go plan Bam's funeral, waiting for Skanes to bring us his bitch," Kesha said tight as hell.

"Wait, what?" Tony asked surprisingly. "What the fuck she do?"

"Somebody told where the fuck we stay and I wanna know who," Kesha said. "And right now, she is the main suspect."

"Are you fucking serious?" Tony asked, standing up too fast. "Ahh Fuck!" he screamed painfully.

"Baby," Kesha said worriedly. "Are you ok?"

"Yeah I'm good," Tony said, catching his breath. "Moving too damn fast. So, what Gripp say at the meeting?"

"They heading to Arkansas this afternoon."

"They? What? Is everyone going?"

"Yes, including Gripp."

"Fuck that!" Tony said, going to the room. "Niggas not going to war and leaving me. Shit, I wanna kill some shit too." Tony pulled a bag out of his closet.

"Nigga if you don't sit your fresh-out-the-hospital ass down somewhere. The only place you going is in that hot tub with me tonight," she said, lowering her tone.

"Now baby you know I can't just sit here while my people go to war; I'm not that nigga."

"And we all know that. Don't worry, we got other things for you to handle."

"Oh yeah, like what?"

"Well first you gotta handle me," she said blushing. "We can talk about the rest afterwards."

"I can dig it," Tony said as the doorbell rang. He went to see who it was.

"Who is that at my house?" Kesha said with a smart tone.

Tony opened the door. "What's the deal, Half Ton? I see you brought that controller."

"Yep and I'm bout to whoop that ass on this Xbox," Half Ton said, walking inside and to the game room.

"Yeah right," Tony responded as he followed him down the hall.

"Umm. Baby?" Kesha said.

"My bad baby," Tony said. "That's Half Ton. "We bout to get on this 2K for a little bit."

"Oh ok. Well, go ahead baby," Kesha said opening the door. "I'm gonna get on in here with Yetta and Ma Williams. I love you."

"I love you too Snicker Butt." Tony said, giggling. "Kiss Ma and Yetta for me."

"Okay, Daddy. Talk to you later," Kesha said hanging up the phone. She got out the car and joined the ladies as they walked into the funeral home.

Gripp was at his house packing a bag while Bee took a shower. She didn't like the idea of him showing his face to unnecessary people, but she understood that, in this game, feelings get put to the side. However, feeling is what she needed.

She turned off the shower and walked to the bedroom, dripping wet. Gripp turned and his eyes opened wide. She smiled.

"Damn, Bee," Gripp said licking his lips. "You look like you got something on your mind?"

"Maybe," she said, walking towards him. As she walked, she glanced and checked the time. *It's three thirty-four*, she thought to herself. *Gives me about fifteen minutes*. She pushed Gripp on the bed and pulled off his sweats.

"Damn baby," Gripp said as he began sucking her nipples. He bit them softly as she got him ready to slide inside her. She got on top and went down until the tip of him was inside her.

She touched his face. "Now we ain't got time for no love making," she said, rubbing his chest with her other hand. "Fuck the shit out of me, Gripp."

"Strong ass legs," Gripp said, noticing she still had just the tip inside her. He pushed a little deeper as she came slowly, making that pussy wet as water. He grabbed her ass and shoved her down onto him.

"OH FUCK!" She screamed as he slowly went in and out of her. He started speeding up his stroke massaging her pussy until she jumped off, rubbing her clit as she squirted all over him.

She sat back down and started riding again, but he had other plans. He picked her up, did a spin, and laid her on her back putting her legs in the air. She grabbed him and put him in as he fell giving her every inch.

"OH MY GOD!" She moaned in ecstasy. She pulled him close. "Fuck me Daddy!"

"With pleasure," he said, pushing in and out. He grabbed her neck and sat back, pulling her up as he continued to pound away.

Her moans were so loud they didn't hear the doorbell ring. She was cuming hard when Gripp's phone rang. They both looked at the clock and it was 3:58.

"Niggas always on time," Gripp said getting up to answer the phone. *Who the fuck calling me from Arkansas?* He thought before he answered. "Who Dis?"

"How the fuck ya bitch ass still alive?" Nick asked, hitting the blunt.

"Now I know you didn't just call my fucking phone!" Gripp said extremely angry. "Bitches got balls now?"

"Now is that any way to talk to ya new boss?" Nick asked, smiling. "It's about time you fall in line while you got a choice. Green not gonna supply you once we knock off ya connect." Nick hit the blunt again.

"Ain't nobody worried bout you pussy ass Niggas," Gripp said, laughing. "You fucked up when you had Bam killed, you pussy!"

Nick got quiet. *What the fuck he talking about? I got Bam killed? He thought to himself.* "See here you go putting bodies where they don't belong," Nick said to Gripp.

"Okay, play stupid," Gripp said, getting up. "I will see you soon." Gripp hung up the phone. He looked at Bee then went back to packing.

"Seriously baby?" she said surprisingly.

"Hell yeah," he said. "I'm gonna kill him and Green bitch ass." He put his sweats and shirt on. After getting shoes from the closet, he grabbed his bag and went downstairs.

The squad was already downstairs with looks in their faces and ready for war. "What's good Fellas?" Gripp said, shaking hands and showing love.

"What's good Boss?" Yella said.

"Shit, it's been a funny day," Gripp said, laughing. "You will never guess who just called me."

"Who?" Doe said, lighting a blunt.

"That asshole, Nick," Gripp said, pouring a shot.

"What the fuck that nigga calling you for?" Yella asked, grabbing the blunt from Doe.

"The nigga say I need to be nice to my new boss cause they gonna take out Ma Williams and I'm gonna have to kiss Green ass." They all shared a good laugh.

"Whatever nigga," Doe said, walking towards the door. "Let's get the fuck on this damn highway." He grabbed his keys and headed outside.

"Alright baby," Gripp turned and said to Bee. "I'll see you when we get back."

"Okay, Daddy," she said, pulling him close. She kissed him long and deep before letting him go. "Be careful. I love you."

"I love you too baby. We out," Gripp said, closing the door. She watched as the squad loaded up and pulled out the driveway.

CHAPTER 6

The driver seen the lights first. "Hey!" he said, turning his head around. "We got company." He pointed at the police lights behind them.

Gripp looked at Doe then at Yella. They both pulled out guns as Doug D grabbed the shotgun from under the seat.

"Pull over," Gripp said, getting his Fold-A-Way Nine from his pocket. He sat back in his seat.

The driver stopped the car; the officer pulled in behind them. They all watched suspiciously as the officer got out of the car and walked towards their car. When the officer got to the driver's window, the driver let down the window, and asked "What seems to be the problem officer?"

"We clocked you doing forty-five in a thirty-five. License and registration," the officer demanded. The driver handed him his information and the officer went back to his cruiser.

The driver turned to look at Gripp and said, "Aye we haven't been in a thirty-five mile per hour zone, He said, I think this is a set up."

After the driver's statement, Doe opened the back door and stepped out of the truck. He looked at the officers with their back turned then Gripp's phone suddenly went off. "Yo?" Gripp said confusedly. "White just texted and said, *get down*!

Yella instantly grabbed Gripp and pushed him to the floor before bullets started flying.

"Yo, get out," Doe yelled, shooting towards the cops. He shot the window out then hit one cop in the leg. The other cop ran to the back of the car to reload.

"Come on!" Doe yelled, pulling Gripp up off the floor. "Let's move."

They all got out of the truck and headed towards the gas station. The cops started shooting again. Yella and Doug D returned fire. His shotgun tore holes in the police car. "WATCH IT!" Doe yelled as he seen the truck pull up. Four dudes jumped out and start blasting. Doug D aimed his piece towards them and let it sing. He hit one guy and pushed him back into the truck.

"Fuck," Marcus yelled. He blasted his AK towards the truck tearing it to pieces. "Tim, BLAST!" Marcus then headed towards the back of the truck.

"FIRE!" Tim yelled, laughing as he threw the grenade at the truck.

Gripp yelled, "Run," and everyone took off seconds before the truck blew. Tim and Marcus instantly got up and started blasting again. When they stopped firing, they didn't see anyone.

"Where the fuck did they go?" Tim asked as they both looked around.

"Right there!" Marcus yelled, pointing towards the corner. "Let's go," he said as they ran after them.

Gripp turned around. "Everybody good?" He asked looking at his squad. They all nodded. Gripp turned and started to walk forward when the two SUVs pulled up. "Are you kidding me?" Gripp reloaded his gun.

Tim and Marcus hit the corner, blasting.

"Yella," Doe yelled, "DUMP!"

Yella fired until the extended clip was empty. "I'm out!" he yelled at Doe.

The doors opened to the SUVS. Blake and Faba Abba got out with Mac 10's blasting the whole street.

"Get in!" Blake yelled to Gripp and the squad. Everyone ran as they held the Baker Brothers back. They stopped shooting and got in the truck. They looked down the street and seen the brothers running the other way. They sped off down the street headed towards I40.

"What the fuck!" Gripp said, looking behind them. "Niggas getting too close."

"Hell yeah they is. Killed the fucking driver!" Doe said, shaking his head. "Good looking out Faba. You niggas right the fuck on time."

"No doubt," Faba said, nodding his head. "Good thing Ma Williams called when she did."

"Ma Williams?" Gripp said. "She called you?"

"Yeah," Faba answered. "She said to get to ya'll as quick as possible so me and Blake did."

"What made her send ya'll?" Gripp asked intrigued.

"Cause that nigga Green called this morning with words," Faba said. "Told her to find a new Distro."

"SON OF A BITCH! Where is she?" Gripp asked, looking for his phone.

"She was leaving the funeral home with Kesha and Yetta when she called me, Faba replied. "Said they were heading to Tony's."

"Yo get to Tony's NOW!" Gripp yelled, pulling out his phone. He dialed Kesha's number.

"Hey Dad," Kesha said when she answered. "What's up? Ya'll on the highway yet?"

"Naw," Gripp said instantly. "Where ya'll at?"

"We almost to the house," Kesha answered. "What's t…" A car suddenly interjects her words as it crashed into her car. She dropped her phone during the collision.

"Princess? Princess? PRINCESS!?" Gripp yelled through the phone. "Speed this Bitch up!" Faba smashed on the gas with Blake going as fast behind him.

Kesha looked up to see if everyone was okay. She turned around to see FeFe walking towards the car. "Hey

Yetta," Kesha said grabbing her gun. "It's a set up." She cocked her 9.

"Fuck!" Yetta said, grabbing Ma Williams. "How many?" She grabbed her gun and handed one to Ma Williams.

"Looks like three," Kesha replied. "You ready?"

"Nope," Yetta responded. "But fuck it! Let's go."

They both got out the car on different sides, blasting. FeFe and her crew ran behind the truck and tried to return fire, but Kesha and Yetta had bullets coming nonstop.

The driver got out and grabbed Ma Williams from the back seat and pulled her to the front of the car. Yetta stopped shooting and reloaded her gun. Kesha started walking towards the car still, blasting. She hit one guy in the head before her gun started clicking.

"Fuck," Kesha said as she turned to run to the car.

FeFe jumped from behind the car blasting as her partner came from the other side. FeFe aimed for Ma Williams and fired but the driver jumped in front of the bullet, killing him instantly.

"I fucking missed," she said, aiming again. Before she could fire, Yetta shot three times, hitting her in the arm and shoulder.

"Got that bitch! Yetta yelled as she fired towards the other guy while he was running away. She turned to check on Ma Williams as Faba and Blake hit the corner. Gripp jumped out before the truck even stopped moving.

"Yo, ya'll good?" Gripp asked as he looked around the scene.

"Yeah," Yetta said. "I got that bitch!" She pointed towards the car.

Gripp walked over to look. "Got who?" Gripp asked, looking at the blood on the ground.

Yetta ran over to the empty spot. "Fuck, that bitch got away! I know I shot FeFe ass." She looked around but didn't see any trace of her. "How the fuck these frails keep finding us?"

"I don't fucking know baby girl," Gripp said, putting his arm around Yetta. "But we bout to end this shit once and for all. Yo, load up. Let's go to Tony's."

They all got in the SUVS and drove off once again leaving the massacre for the city to clean up. They made it to the house a few minutes later to find Tony and Half Ton standing by his Lincoln. When they parked and got out, Tony's eyes instantly got big.

"What the fuck?" he said running to Kesha and Yetta. "What the hell happened?" He grabbed his girls and held them tight before getting Ma Williams out of the car.

Gripp looked at Tony and said, "Niggas came hard but *KILLA CITY* still standing. Now it's time to go tear up some of they shit."

He turned and walked in the house. Everyone followed. They all sat in the living room. Tony's doorbell rang and they all grabbed guns. "Chill ya'll," Tony said, opening the door. "It's just Nine Milli."

"What's good?" Nine said. "It look like ya'll been in Iraq. What happened?"

Gripp threw a roll of paper towels at him. "Shut up," he said as he poured a shot.

"I'm bout tired of this bullshit," Kesha said, pacing. "How many fucking losses we gonna take before we kill these niggas?"

"What you mean we?" Doug D asked, looking at Kesha. "You not going with us."

Kesha looked at Doug D with despair and asked, "What the fuck you say to me nigga?" Kesha turned her body towards Doug D.

"I said you not going," Doug D repeated.

Kesha's face got tight as she licked her lips. Gripp and Tony slid to the bar and sat down. They both knew she was about to snap.

"Yeah that's what I thought you said," Kesha said as she walked up to him and touched his face with her left hand. He looked at her hand before he felt the steel behind his right ear. "Now normally I would shoot your foot or hand, but since we at war and we might need your loudmouth ass; I'm gonna give you a pass just this one time."

"Pass," Doug D said, looking at Gripp. "This shit…" Kesha put her finger over his mouth, and everyone shared a quiet laugh.

"I see you didn't pay attention before because it didn't sound like the words I wanna hear," Kesha said as she cocked her gun. “Bitch, I’m Gripp’s Princess!” She pressed the gun harder into his ear. “I do what the fuck I want.”

“Kesha! ENOUGH!” Ma Williams yelled. Kesha put down the gun and walked to stand beside Ma Williams. “Gripp.” Ma Williams nodded her head at Gripp.

“Check this, we gonna split and do a sneak hit. Bus, Train, and Plane. We gonna come down on these frails like today is tomorrow ya dig. Tony, go ahead.”

Tony said, “Aight. So Gripp hit me this morning and I had my man Black find out some shit. I got four targets that we need to hit. Nick is strong in muscle but not in funds. Green is the bank and wants a profit on his investment.”

Everybody laughed. “NOISE!” Doe said to the room. “Go ahead Tony.”

“My nigga,” Tony said, laughing. “The dude don’t even wanna work for Green, he just wants power. We take his bank; we take his power. That simple.”

“Shit and take the bank,” Yella said. “I love those words together.”

“Yeah,” Faba said. “Taking his bank is cool but what about the Baker Brothers? They most likely were paid at least half up front otherwise they wouldn’t be coming so hard.”

Gripp thought about that for a second. “You know you got a point Faba. So that means we gotta sneak up on them Niggas as well,” he said.

Ma Williams stood up. “I will deal with the Baker Brothers,” she said, nodding to Blake. Blake had a confused look on his face, remembering that his other gun is in Arkansas with Pain. “What is it?” she asked.

“You forget Big Rick is still in Arkansas,” Blake answered.

Ma looked around to see who would back up Blake.

“Don’t trip Cuddy,” Half Ton said, stepping in the room. “I fucks with Gripp. I’ll watch your back.” Half Ton reached for Tony’s Fold-A-Way.

“Already,” Blake said, nodding to Ma Williams. “It’s a bet.”

“Bet. Now this is how we gonna do this,” Gripp spoke. “Me and Doe going after Nick. Doug D, you and Nine Milli go after that bitch Green. I’m gonna have Pain stir up some shit in Arkansas so everyone thinks we are there. Move in the shadows. Think smart and stay invisible.

“Aye,” Yetta said interrupting Gripp. “Saturday at 12:00 we will be laying my baby to rest. I don’t give a fuck what the hell going on, everybody better be back in *KILLA CITY* by then.” Everyone got quiet as Yetta looked them in their faces.

“Matter fact, where the fuck is Skanes?” Yella asked, breaking the silence.

“Man, that’s a grown ass man dog,” Doug D said. “And last time I checked we don’t report to you.”

“Shut ya bubble head ass up D,” Yella said as everyone laughed.

"Aight," Gripp said. "Let's move. Time to make it hot."

"MONEY!" everyone yelled as they walked outside.

Gripp turned to look at Tony. "What?" Tony asked confusedly. "Oh, hell naw, ya'll ain't taking any of my whips!"

"What you expect us to all ride in one truck?" Faba sarcastically asked. "Naw, run them keys bruh."

"Fuck that, niggas better call Uber," Tony said, walking in the house. He came out two minutes later with keys and a remote. "Come on, shit." He walked to the garage in the back. He stopped in front of the garage and hit the button.

"Now that's what the fuck I'm talking bout, Tony," Gripp said, looking and pointing at the custom, green and black, *KILLA CITY* bubble Chevy on black 26" rims. "Let me get that."

Faba went over to the Phantom that Ma Williams bought Tony for making a million dollars before he graduated.

"Fucking book smart ass nigga," Faba said, leaning on the car.

Yella jumped in the 2017 Ford F150 on 28's.

"Chromed out for no damn reason," he said while Doug D took one of Tony's motorcycles.

"I tell ya'll what while you all ooohh wee with my shit, I know where all you niggas keep a stash if anything, and I do mean anything, happen to any of my whips," Tony said as he threw everyone keys before he turned and walked back in the house.

Faba opened the back door to the Phantom so Ma Williams and Yetta could get in. She turned to Kesha and said, "We will see you in the morning. Make sure you relax, and my son as well." She turned and got in as Faba closed the door.

Half Ton got in on the other side while Faba and Blake got in the front. Gripp backed out first then sped down the driveway. He stopped mid point and turned to look at the house and just as he thought, Tony was looking out the window. He laughed. "Doe pass me a blunt," Gripp commanded. Doe laughed as he handed the blunt to Gripp. He hit the blunt then turned to wave at Tony as he smashed on the gas down the driveway. Everyone else just cruised down the paved road.

illa City

CHAPTER 7

Kesha went inside the house and closed the front door. She shut her eyes and took a deep breath. When she exhaled, a tear fell down her face. She reached out her hand to wipe it, but Tony beat her to it. “Hey,” he said, wiping her tears away. “Come here.” Looking at her with protective eyes, he grabbed her and held her in his arms tight.

“Baby,” she said looking him in his eyes. “What if we don’t make it out of this whole?”

“Now we ain’t got time to think like that baby,” he replied, picking her up. “This is the game. We knew what we signed up for before we knew what we signed up for.”

“I know but look at what we have lost over the years,” she said, laying her head on his chest. “And this time we’re dealing with someone who thinks he knows how we move.”

Tony walked up the stairs thinking about what Kesha said. “You know what baby, you just gave me a hell of an idea," he said, walking Kesha into the room and sitting her on the bed.

"What's that baby?" she asked, putting the pillow behind her head.

"Like you said, he thinks he knows how we move, right? So maybe it's time we think like he moves," Tony said, walking to the bathroom. He started running the water in the tub. He went under the sink to grab some bubbles.

"What you mean baby?" Kesha asked, trying to look and see what he was doing.

"Well one thing we know is he wants power, Tony said taking off his shirt. And we know how Arkansas move. Power must be shown. War or no war."

He went back to the bathroom and turned off the water. He untied his shorts and took them off. He positioned his drawers so that the lines leading to his shaft would show. He tapped the head of his dick to wake him up. He stood looking at himself in the mirror to make sure his bulge looked good enough to eat before he turned towards the door.

When he walked out, Kesha looked at him with lustful eyes, "Damn daddy," and licked her lips. "What are you doing?"

"Being that nigga," he said as he grabbed her hand and led her to the bathroom. He turned and started undressing her. They both looked at each other for an intense amount of time before Tony broke the silence.

“Come on baby.” He got into the tub. He sat back so that she could sit in front of him.

“Yes, Daddy,” she said, stepping into the tub. The warm sensation of the water, mixed with her wonderful man, made her instantly moist. She sat down and leaned back on him. He wrapped his arms around her and held her tight.

“You good baby?” he asked, kissing her ear.

“I am now,” she said as she turned and kissed him. She turned and relaxed her body back onto him. She enjoyed hearing nothing but his breathing. Her mind somehow lingered back to her college days. The times they had and how the crew stood strong until this nigga killed Bam. Her fist got tight.

“Naw baby, Tony said touching her hand. “Anger doesn’t move us. Remember that. You know Bam was my guy too and trust *KILLA CITY* gonna handle that.”

Kesha relaxed her hands and laughed. “Get out of my head. She said slapping his chest.

They sat in the tub, enjoying the water for a while before getting out and going to the bed. As they got into bed Tony thought back to how close Kesha, Yetta, and MaStarPeace were back in the day. Bam was like the big protector then, to his sister and her crew.

“Bad Ass Mama,” he laughed aloud from his thought.

“What’s so funny?” she asked, looking up to him.

“Thinking about you and your crazy click,” he answered, pulling the covers over their bodies. “Have you talked to MaStarPeace yet?”

“Naw, not yet. I don’t even know what to say to her,” Kesha said, shaking her head. “I mean, what do you say to someone who lost their brother to the game she didn’t want any of us to be a part of?”

Tony sat back. To him, the game is what it is. He said, “I don’t know baby, but I can’t think about that right now. We at war and someone gonna die over Bam. She may not be part of the game, but she know what it is.”

“Yeah I know she do,” Kesha said. “But that don’t make it any easier.” She reached and turned out the light.

“Naw baby,” Tony said. “It doesn’t.” He kissed her neck. “Go to sleep. We will deal with it in the morning.”

“OK Daddy,” she said as she sat up. We will but right now you got another problem.

“Oh yeah, he said looking at her, and what’s That?”

She threw the covers on the floor as she got on top of him. Her eyes and said all the words needed. She leaned and kissed his neck as her hands explored.

“Now this is a problem I can solve. Tony said as he palmed her ass tight as she moved her hips. Kesha?” He said.

She kissed him deeply still not saying a word. Her lips left his as she continued to kiss his body. He moaned as her tongue made circles around his nipples. She went down and licked his belly as she stroked his dick.

She stopped and looked at him. “Put your hands behind your head.” She said.

He looked at her but did what she said. She kissed the path to his shaft as she used her tongue to tease him. Still stroking his dick, she wrapped her lips around the head.

“Oh, shit baby! He said moaning. DAMN…

She took him in deeper slowly stroking and moving her head until he touched the back of her throat. She continued sucking him making his moans get louder.

She slowed down sucking him slow as she turned her body and sat her pussy on his face. She opened her legs so he could get his tongue deeper inside her. She moved her hips while grinding and fucking his face.

She stroked his dick as she played with his balls making him hard as a rock. “Oh, fuck baby, she screamed, I’m cumming!" she said as she raised up and squirted all over his face.

“My, my, my girl, he said licking his lips, them juices taste good. They both laughed as she crawled and set him inside her as he slapped her ass from the back.

Oh, fuck Daddy!!! She moaned as she bounced her ass in a fast pace motion. SHIT!” she screamed. Right as she was about to cum, he pushed her off him and grabbed the back of her hair as he shoved his dick deep inside her. He continued to hit it hard as she screamed and moaned.

"Give it to me Daddy!! She screamed filling his dick jump for joy as he came inside her. They both fell on the bed.

"No fair, she said smiling, that wasn't about you."

"I know you, he said wrapping his arms around her, all you want is that good nutt. He laughed.

"Whatever, she said rubbing his arms, I love you big head. "

"I love you too, he said closing his eyes, now go to sleep.

CHAPTER 8

Pain and Big Rick were sitting in Club 1504 having a drink when Pain's phone rang. He looked at it and seen it was Gripp.

"Hold on Gripp," Pain said when he answered the phone. "Let me get somewhere I can hear you." He went into the bathroom stall and closed the door. "What's good?"

"Pain, what's good son," Gripp asked. "Where the hell you at?"

"Chilling in Club 1504, having a drink with Big Rick. Bout to head to our rooms here in a few. Why, ya'll here?"

"Naw," Gripp responded. "That's what I'm calling about. We changed things up a little bit. I need you to do something."

"What's that, Boss?"

"Stir up some shit so everyone thinks we are already there; make sure it's loud and trouble. We gonna bring out the bitch in niggas."

Pain had a good laugh at that one. He knew Gripp had a thing for surprising people. "Aight Pops," he said. "You know I can handle that with ease." He heard the club get loud.

"What's going on there tonight?" Gripp said, hearing the club through the phone.

"Big OG in town. Supposed to be doing a concert in Crime Bluff Thursday night."

"Big OG? Who? Concert?"

"YEP," Pain said, laughing.

"So, you telling me my nigga Yung TutZilla in town?"

"Yeah, he just walked in the club. He may come get at me in a bit, I'll tell him you said what's up."

"Yeah do that, you say the concert is in Crime Bluff?"

"Hell yeah and you know that's neutral territory so we can't pop off there. Plus, it's TutZilla's homecoming. Shit, Crime Bluff need this concert."

"It's cool. I wouldn't fuck up shit for da homie anyway, but *KILLA CITY* will be in da building ya dig?"

"Already boss. I'll get with ya cuz."

"Gone," Gripp concluded, ending the call.

Pain left the bathroom and went back to the VIP section. He sat down, turned to Big Rick and said, "Yo check this, I just got off the phone with Gripp; he wants us to stir up some shit, so people think they in town." Pain lit a blunt.

"So, what, they not coming?"

"Yeah they coming, but Gripp has a thing for surprising people, so I say we start a fire or two."

Big Rick laughed loud and hard. So loud that Yung TutZilla heard him and started walking toward their table.

"*KILLA CITY* in the building!" TutZilla said showing love. "What up Pain? Big Rick? What the hell ya'll doing in Da Rock?"

"Fam we in town for your concert," Pain said, lying as he stood up. "We just here to turn up." Pain started dancing.

TutZilla laughed and said, "I see you still a damn fool. So, I hear ya'll at war?" TutZilla noticed both of their reactions.

"Well," Pain said rubbing his head. "I wouldn't call it war OG, it's more like you fuck with the wrong one and we gonna spank that ass."

"I can dig that," TutZilla said. "Let me tell you something though, that nigga Nick worth more to you alive than he is dead."

"Alive?" Big Rick said. "Bahumbug my nigga. Ain't no alive after them niggas killed Bam? Not one breath."

"What you mean Bam got killed?" TutZilla asked, looking confused.

"Yeah," Pain answered. "Nick hired the Baker Brothers and they killed Bam at Tony's two nights ago. I really don't see Yetta or my sister letting that ride. Hell, Bam's sister not gonna let it ride and she's the good one."

"Man damn," TutZilla said shaking his head. "Well I won't speak on it unless it gets to that point. But if it does and I call a meeting, I don't wanna hear shit Ya Dig?"

"Yeah OG," Pain said, showing respect to a King. "You won't hear shit."

TutZilla got up and shook Pain's hand and asked, "See you niggas at the concert?"

"Fuck yeah! *KILLA CITY* in the building," Pain said once again, laughing. "Support is real fam."

"Oh, is the KING showing his face?" TutZilla asked. "Haven't seen my nigga in years. When he gonna get in town?"

"SHIIIIDD ya guess is as good as mine," Pain said, laughing. "You know Gripp."

"Indeed," TutZilla said. "I'll hit that nigga up later. Love." TutZilla gave them a quick handshake before he went back to the crowd that was still screaming his name.

He went on the stage and grabbed the mic. "SO YA'LL WANT TUTZILLA?" The crowd went crazy. "WELL YA GOT HIM!" The beat to *HOTTEST IN THE CITY* came on and Tutzilla tore up the stage.

"Man, it's amazing how far a nigga can go," Big Rick said. "Look at our nigga on stage shining."

"I can dig it bruh," Pain said. "But that's his calling. We killas, so we shine threw his music. Remember da hood is everywhere my nigga."

"Mane, bring your goofy ass on, Big Rick said laughing. Let's go start some shit."

"Fuck you nigga," Pain said, laughing. "Grab that bottle though." They both laughed as they left the club and got into the truck. Big Rick poured them a drink while Pain rolled a blunt.

"So, you got a plan or we just fucking up shit?" Big Rick asked.

"Bruh we just gonna fuck up some shit," Pain answered as he hit the blunt. "I say we hit em where it hurts the most."

"THE CASINO!" they both said. Big Rick put the car in drive and headed towards the east end of Little Rock.

Ced's Casino was the hottest spot in the city. It stayed packed, with a live crowd. It was also the hub for Green's money.

They made it to the casino parking lot and found a place to park. Pain pulled out his phone and checked the time. It was 11:14pm. He dialed Janae's number.

"What's good, Pain?" she asked when she picked up. "You straight?"

"I'm a hundred baby girl," Pain said with a soft voice. "Ya'll still in Da Rock?"

"Yeah," Janae said, smiling. "April wanted to hit the casino before we went back to Crime Bluff. We bout to leave here in a few though. What's up?"

"Looking at it," Pain replied. "It's a good thing you at the casino though. Now I don't have to wait on you."

"What?" she asked confusedly. "What the hell you on nigga?"

"We bout to fuck this fucking casino up, after we rob it, of course."

"Hold up," she said waving her hand like he could see her through the phone. "So, you think you gonna walk into Green's casino, rob it, then fuck it up and live to tell about it?"

"You fucking right," Pain said with his chest. "Girl you better act like you know."

"Well I guess I'm bout to find out what the Prince of *KILLA CITY* can do."

"You see any familiar faces in there tonight?" Pain asked while rolling a blunt.

"A few; Nick, J Rich, and Smooth The Dude were here, but they left bout fifteen minutes ago. Green and Ced still here and I think I seen Boney and Tippy but not in a minute," she said looking around the room.

"Bet," Pain said as he and Big Rick got out the car. "Keep ya head low." He hung up the phone as they walked in the entrance of the casino.

"You see this bruh," Big Rick asked. "Legal drugs; fucking slot machines." He shook his head. "You ready my nigga?"

"Fuck yeah," Pain answered, pulling the toys out of his bag. "There go the ladies." Pain waved them over. "Ya'll good?"

"Gucci," Corey replied. "What ya'll on?"

Big Rick laughed and answered, "Fuck it up, Fuck it up." He danced.

"Ya'll might wanna head towards the door," Pain said, pulling the pin from a grenade. April looked at him for a moment before Janae grabbed her arm and started walking. He turned and threw the grenade towards the bar area.

As soon as it blew, the crowd instantly started running towards the door. Big Rick and Pain fired shots in the air as they rushed to the money room. They stopped when they saw Boney and Tippy coming out. They walked right past them heading towards the exit.

Pain came from behind the slot machine and went to the door. He pulled another pin and dropped the grenade by the door then ran back behind the machine. When it blew, Big Rick ran in first.

He shot the table they were counting on. "Get the fuck on the ground," he yelled to J Poole.

Poole just sat there then raised his head to look at Pain and said, "Pain Loc." He reached out his hand. "Why the fuck ya'll doing this shit? You know this is Green's shit."

"What up J Poole?" Pain said, shaking his hand. "You know we at war with his bitch ass. Plus, him and Nick had Bam killed and we getting blood."

"Wait?" J Poole said, looking at Ced. "What you mean they had Bam killed? Man tell me you playing?"

"Real shit, fam, so don't take this personal," Pain said as he looked at Big Rick. "Get that bread yo."

Ced stood up as Big Rick was filling up a trash bag full of his money. "Look, we gonna let you walk out of here out of respect for Bam and MaSTARpeace but this is gonna have to be answered for. You sure you want those problems?"

"Let em *Knuck if they Buck*," Pain said. "Gripp stay ready."

"I hope so cause Shine and Tyson ain't gonna like this shit," Ced said as he sat down and poured a shot. "Let me drink this before you shoot, Big Rick."

"Shoot?" Big Rick said, laughing. "Man, folks you not gonna die tonight, can't deliver our message if you dead." He looked at Pain.

"Message?" J Poole said, lighting a blunt. "What Message?"

Pain leaned down closer to J Poole and said, "Tell that bitch ass boss of yours that Gripp in town and *KILLA CITY* took his shit." He stood up and turned towards the door. He stopped.

"What Nigga?" J Poole said, looking at Pain.

"That shit smell bomb as fuck," Pain said, reaching for the blunt. "Let me hit that."

"Here nigga," J Poole said, passing it. Pain hit that shit and instantly tasted the flavor.

"Damn," he said giving it back. "That's some good shit there boy."

"Well you know Boney and Tippy keep that Kelly Roland. Go ahead, I got more." He said waving the blunt away.

"What is it with these names," Pain said, looking at Big Rick. "Remember that shit we smoked on the way here was Half Ton's Yonce'. Good ass weed though. Let's ride, Big Rick."

They both walked out the casino with people still fighting to get out of the exits. As they got in the car, Pain pulled out his phone to text Gripp, not paying attention to the niggas walking up to the car. Pain turned to the gun pointed at his head.

Killa City

CHAPTER 9

When Tony woke up the next morning, he rolled over and felt that his bed was empty. He got up and put on his Dallas Cowboys' robe and went to the bathroom. After handling his business, he went downstairs. He found Kesha sitting on the couch in the living room.

"Good morning, beautiful," he said as he kissed her on the cheek. "What you doing up so early? I see you done pulled out the albums, huh?"

"Yeah," Kesha said, smiling. "Looking back at our young days." She laughed. "Look at us." She handed him a picture of her, Yetta, and MaStarPeace, standing in front of the University of Oklahoma's stadium.

"Hell Yeah. The BAM! Bad and Mature. I like how ya'll named the squad after his ass," Tony said, laughing.

"That's because he was our bodyguard even though we were all bad as hell. Especially MaStarPeace ass. You know our freshman year at OU, he broke some guy phone for taking a picture of her and, when dude got mad, he broke his jaw."

"Seriously? That's crazy. That's why I'm glad I went to UAPB, cause I would've killed one of them niggas 'bout my sister. Especially, when she was fucking with that nigga Nick. Shit came back to bite us in the ass."

"Now, at first he was a great guy and she fell for him hard, but it was always toxic," Kesha said, turning the page.

"Toxic? What you mean by that?" Tony asked, looking confused.

Kesha looked at her man and realized that Yetta never told him. She pulled out a picture and said, "Look at ya'll though." She handed it to Tony, changing the subject.

"Fuck yeah," he said, smiling. He looked at the first picture they took as *KILLA CITY*. "This was after I brought Yella down for Bedlam that one year, when Ma introduced me to Gripp and when I found out who you really were." He gave her a look.

"Whatever," she said, laughing. "You knew me and who my dad is, but it didn't matter then or now." She smiled. "Didn't want you running away because I'm Gripp's Princess ya dig?" She leaned over and kissed him.

"Aight. I dig it," Tony said as he got up and went to the kitchen to make some coffee. When he came back Kesha was getting up. "What you about to do?"

"It's time to go see MaStarPeace. She got a show today on campus, I figured I'd go take her to lunch and chat."

"Already," he said, grabbing her hand. "You got this baby." He kissed her then turned to walk upstairs.

"OK," she said, grabbing her keys. "I love you and I will see you later."

"I love you too baby," Tony said. "And tell MaStarPeace cute ass I said what's up." He laughed.

"Alright nigga," Kesha said, giggling. "I done told you. I know all my friends B.A.M. but watch ya mouth." She closed the door."

She got in Bam's 300 and started it. Blocc Breed began playing through the speakers. "Damn I miss you bruh," Kesha said to herself, wiping the tear from her eye. She put the car in drive and headed towards OSU, Oklahoma City.

When she pulled up, her mind drifted to how long she'd gone to school, off and on. Maybe one day she would focus more and finish. She parked and went inside the auditorium. She walked in the school studio and sat on the couch as MaStarPeace was doing her interview with TRE DAY.

"So MaStarPeace," TRE DAY began. "Your poetry has sparked the world, and everyone is wondering what's next."

"Well," MaStarPeace started. "Next is gonna be a little break for me. See I lost my brother recently and I think I need some time to process it so I'm gonna spend the next couple of days with my family and my girls." She seen Kesha and waved at her.

"Yeah, we are so sorry for your loss. You know you will be in our prayers," TRE DAY said, passing her a rose. She smiled. To brighten the mood, TRE DAY changed the subject. "But on another note that show you did last night was off the chain! Really digging the way, you came in the building. Obviously these two are everywhere you go." He pointed at Richard and Alex.

"You know I rep that good ol' Delta Sigma Theta Sorority, Inc. and I love that song Boo'ed UP, so everywhere I go I gotta stayed QUE'D up," she said laughing.

"Aight. I see ya. I'm quite sure they keep stupid away," TRE DAY said, laughing.

"Trust, these Doggs protect the Bad And Mature," she said, looking at her bodyguards.

"Well this is for them; this is TRE DAY with the lovely MaStarPeace, signing out with Atomic Dog for the Que Doggs."

They took off the headphones as the record began to play. Richard and Alex stepped out the booth and stood with Kesha while MaStarPeace finished up. She came out thc booth and instantly ran to her girl's arms.

"Oh my God girl I have missed you," MaStarPeace said, holding Kesha tight.

“I miss you too girl,” Kesha said as they sat on the couch. “It’s been way too long, and I hate it’s under these circumstances. I’m so sorry we let this happen.” She wiped away her tears.

“Girl…,” MaStarPeace said as she looked at the floor. “I feel so numb without my brother here. I keep watching all our videos over and over. She picked her head up to look at Kesha. “What happened to my brother?”

Kesha just looked at MaStarPeace. “Well it’s people stepping to Gripp. They shot Tony and, while Bam was getting clothes at our house, they got him too.” Kesha put her head down.

“So, who are they?” MaStarPeace said, pointing at Richard. He gave her a nod.

“Naw MaStarPeace, this ain’t for you,” Kesha said, looking at Richard and Alex. “TRUST, *KILLA CITY* gonna handle this.”

MaStarPeace thought for a second and with a serious face said, “Look Kesha, I love you, but ya’ll better get them bitches before I do.”

“Oh, you hard now, huh?” Kesha said, laughing. “Girl come here.” She hugged her friend as the tears came down her face. She finally brought her head from Kesha’s shoulder.

“I’m just pissed the fuck off. How’s Yetta?”

“Honestly she is lost right now,” Kesha said. “You know it’s Nick ass coming at us.”

"That cold hearted bastard," MaStarPeace said with rage in her eyes. "We should've let her kill that nigga."

"Girl, if we knew then what we know now, I would've told Tony about it," Kesha said before she put her hand to her mouth.

"What?" MaStarPeace asked. "You didn't tell Tony? He gonna kick all our butt's for that shit Kesha."

"Yeah I know; let's go get Yetta and go eat."

Skanes was sitting on the couch watching the news. He knew by now that they were wondering where the hell he was. Deanna walked in and sat on the couch beside him. When she touched his arm, he jumped up.

"Don't fucking touch me with ya stupid ass," Skanes said, wiping off his arm.

"Why the fuck you talking to me like that?"

"Really?" Skanes asked, looking at her funny. "You sit there with that smirk on your face like you ain't did shit?"

"What you talking about?" she asked, reaching for her phone. "I ain't did shit." She unlocked her phone and began to make a call until Skanes slapped the phone out of her hand.

"This ain't the time for you to be on the damn phone," he said, getting heated. "We know you been running your mouth to that bitch Green who apparently is your fucking dad."

Deanna just sat on the couch with a blank look on her face. She knew she was caught. "I gotta use the bathroom," she said, getting up from the couch.

"That's all you got to fucking say?" he asked, standing up. "After all I've done for you this is how you do me? This is how you do the crew?"

"What you want me to say?" she asked, looking into his eyes. "It wasn't by choice. I don't fuck with my dad or his people. That's why I left Memphis. When I went back a few months ago, I met him for lunch. He invited me to a birthday party for one of his wife's kids, so I went. I got tired and fell asleep and they got my phone and put a tracker on it and pinned every place I stopped at for the last few months."

"Bitch please! You stay on your fucking phone. How the hell can anybody put something on it and you not know? Go ahead, I'll wait."

"Fucking apps," she answered, shaking her head. "When you bought me this new phone last week the lady asked if I wanted the app transferred to the new phone. I looked and said 'no, doesn't the new phone have a calculator?' She tells me that it's a 'tracker app.' At first, I thought it was you till Bam got killed, that's when I put two and two together."

Skanes sat back down on the couch in disbelief and said, "This shit just unbelievable. I mean, it's just too stupid for you to fucking make up."

"Baby," she said, sitting by him. "I promise you that is really what happen."

"FUCK," Skanes said, rising and grabbing his keys. "Go get ya shit. I gotta get you out of town until I can clear this shit up."

"Clear it up?" She asked confusedly. "Fuck that. I'm not going nowhere."

"Oh, you going," Skanes said, giving her that look. "Now get the fuck up." He reached down and tried to grab her arm, but she got up and ran to the other side of the room.

"I'm not leaving," she said, folding her arms. "What part of that don't you understand nigga?"

"Look, either you get ya shit and get in the fucking car or you can stay and take ya chances with Kesha and Yetta," he said, walking towards the door.

"Wait," she said, running up to him. "What you mean Kesha and Yetta? What they got to do with me?"

"Your stupidity got Bam killed; that ain't something they gonna forgive," he said as he touched her shoulder. "You basically living on borrowed time right now so shut up and let's go before they find us."

"Alright, I'll get some stuff." She turned and walked in the bedroom. Ten minutes later, she came out with a suitcase. "I'm ready."

"Good," he said, grabbing her bags. "Let's go." They walked outside and got in the car. When he started it, he noticed his gas was low. “We gotta stop by the gas station before we hit the highway.”

“Where we going, anyway?” she asked, looking for her phone. “And where’s my phone?”

“Here,” he said, handing her the phone. “And we’re going. That’s all you need to know. He put the car in drive and left the house.

CHAPTER 10

"This is a nice ass truck," Kesha said, looking at the inside of MaStarPeace's SUV.

"Girl, you can thank Richard for that one," MaStarPeace said, looking at Richard. "He got this for me for graduation."

"What you mean he got it for you?" Yetta asked, joking. "What you give him?"

"I didn't have to give him anything," she said, playing with her hair. "He already has MaStarPeace." They all laughed. Richard and Alex both threw up the Que's Hooks to a passing fraternity brother.

"Aye we need to stop by the gas station," Richard said, turning on his signal.

"Good," MaStarPeace said. "I need some gum anyway."

"And I gotta pee so hurry up," Kesha said, putting her phone in her purse.

"Hit that hood store on Tenth and Council," Alex said. "I want some chicken."

"Bet," Richard said, heading to towards the store. They made it there a few minutes later. He parked at pump three. Everyone got out the truck and headed into the store.

"What's up Ronnie?" Kesha asked as they walked in the door.

"What's going on, ladies?" Ronnie asked, coming around the counter. "The look on them faces say ya'll want some chicken.

"You know we do," Kesha said, pointing towards the strips. "Go ahead and fix me up. I'm gonna go use the restroom."

"Me too," Yetta said, following Kesha to the restroom.

"Alright," Ronnie said, fixing up plates. "I got you." He looked at Richard and Alex. "What can I get for you fellas?"

"Yeah," Alex said quickly. "Let me get a four-piece-wing special with fries."

Richard laughed, "Yo let me get a three-piece-chicken strip meal Dogg. Some okra too." He turned to MaStarPeace. "You want anything love?"

"Yeah I'll take a wing meal," MaStarPeace answered, grabbing a lemonade drink out of the freezer.

"Let me get ya'll fixed up," Ronnie said, going to work.

"You gonna feed me after we get some gas?" Deanna asked, rubbing her stomach.

"You can get some chicken at Da Store while I get some gas," Skanes said, turning right on 10th street. He pulled in at pump one and parked.

"You want me to pay for the gas while I'm in there, baby?"

"Yeah," he said, handing her some money. "And get me some wings and a drink."

"What you want, a lemonade?" she asked, opening her door.

"Yeah," he said, viewing the truck in front of him. "And a pack of gum. Damn that truck is nice." He pointed at the truck.

"Yeah it is," she said, getting out the car. "I'll be back." She closed the door and walked inside the store. When she made it to the door, Richard and Alex were coming out.

"How you doing?" Alex said, holding the door open for Deanna.

"I'm good," she said, smiling and walking in. "Such a gentleman. Thank you." She smiled as she watched them walk to that nice truck. She turned and walked to the kitchen to order her food.

"Hey, Ms. D," Ronnie said, smiling. "How you doing today?"

"I'm good, Ronnie," she said, scanning the food. "What you got good back there?"

"Shit, everything good," Ronnie said boastful. "You know how I get down." He put some orders in a bag then turned to drop some more chicken in the fryer.

MaStarPeace walked to the register to sit down some drinks. *Damn, Kesha must have had to shit*, she said to herself, laughing before going back to the kitchen to grab their food.

"Those some nice boots," Deanna said, looking at MaStarPeace as she walked up. "I can't walk in heels like that." They both laughed.

"Thanks," MaStarPeace said. "I try. What's up Ronnie, you got us ready?"

"Yes ma'am," he said, giving her the bags and a ticket. "Just take this to the register."

"Aight," she said, grabbing the bag. "Have a good day." She turned and started walking towards the register.

"You too," Ronnie said, waving. "Come see us next time you in town."

"Will do," she said, turning to the register as Kesha and Yetta came out of the restroom.

Kesha saw Deanna. "Yetta," Kesha said, touching her arm. "There go that bitch Deanna right there."

Yetta looked and walked to Deanna. "Aye bitch," she called. "Come here."

Deanna looked to see who was talking. Her eyes got big when she seen Yetta coming towards her. "Oh Shit," she said, running towards the door.

"Aye you forgot your chicken," Ronnie told Deanna right before MaStarPeace tripped her and made her hit the door.

"I knew you looked familiar," MaStarPeace said, looking at her on the floor. "Get the fuck up."

"Yo," Deanna said, getting up. "It's not what ya'll think. I didn't have…." she was interrupted by Yetta's hand going across her face. Ronnie ran up to try and stop the fight until Kesha held up her hand.

"Naw Ronnie," Kesha said, opening the door. "This here is *KILLA CITY* business. Fall back." She looked at Yetta. "You good sis?"

"Let me kill this bitch," Yetta said.

"Not here," Kesha said. "Let's take her to the house."

"The house?" MaStarPeace said, looking confused. "Why would we take her there?"

"Because one of our best got hit at my house," she said, looking at Deanna. "I wanna know what else her mouth has said."

"Wait," MaStarPeace said, holding up her hand. "I gotta grab our food. She turned back to the counter to get the bags. "Fuck that, I'm hungry."

Skanes looked up and seen them walking out the store. *FUCK!* He said to himself, reaching in the car and grabbing his gun. "Aye Kesha," he said running to them. "What the fuck?"

"What you mean what the fuck?" Kesha asked, irritated. "Yetta told you to bring this bitch to her and obviously you didn't listen. So what? You going against Gripp now? Against me?"

"Man Kesha, it's not what you think. It's more to the shit than you know."

"See," Kesha said, looking at MaStarPeace. "I told you." She started walking towards the truck. Skanes jumped in front of her.

"Naw," Skanes said, pulling out his gun. "Ya'll aint doing this, Kesha. That's my girl."

"Nigga do it look like we give a fuck," Yetta said, walking up to Skanes. "Right now, ain't the time Skanes." She stepped closer. "Now get the fuck out of the way." She pushed him aside and started to walk away until Skanes grabbed her arm.

"I ain't fucking playing with ya'll," he said, squeezing her arm tight. "This is a decision only Gripp can make and I don't see him here."

"Look," MaStarPeace said, holding up her hand and stopping Richard and Alex from coming over. "I don't know you, but there are three things I do know. One, get your fucking hands off my sister." She shoved his arm. "Two, this bitch you call your girl had something to do with my brother's death."

"You Bam sister huh?" Skanes asked, realizing who he was talking to.

"Yeah," MaStarPeace said, pulling out a red 22. "And three, that bitch right there is Gripp's Princess and she don't need his permission to do shit. Now get your mutha fucking ass out the damn way." She pushed him to the side and, even though he didn't move, she turned and grabbed Deanna by the arm. "Come on bitch," She dragged her to the truck. Skanes tried to reach for her but MaStarPeace moved fast. She turned and shot him in the leg.

"AHHHHH you lil short ass bitch!" Skanes said, holding his leg. "Ya'll fucking with the wrong one. He reached for his gun."

"No no no little squirrel," KI said, rushing up. "Let me get that up out ya." He reached down and picked up the gun. "What's up Kesha. Hey, Yetta?"

"What's good KI?" Yetta asked, walking up to hug her friend. "Where the hell you come from?"

"Shit on my way to holla at Kinfolks," KI said, looking at the gun. "I seen ya'll while I was at the light, so I pulled up. Can I keep this shit?" He pointed at the gun.

"Yeah," Yetta answered. "We gotta go."

"Aight, bet," KI concluded, checking the chamber. "Ya'll want me to handle this nigga?"

"Naw," Kesha replied. "That nigga still family." She walked on to the truck as MaStarPeace followed, still dragging Deanna behind her.

"Yo Yetta," KI said, hugging her. "Sorry bout Bam. He was a HYPHY ass nigga."

“Respect my friend. Thank you,” she said, hugging him back. “The funeral is Saturday ok?”

“Already,” KI said. “I got you.” He made sure they all got in the car safe before getting in his impala.

BAM

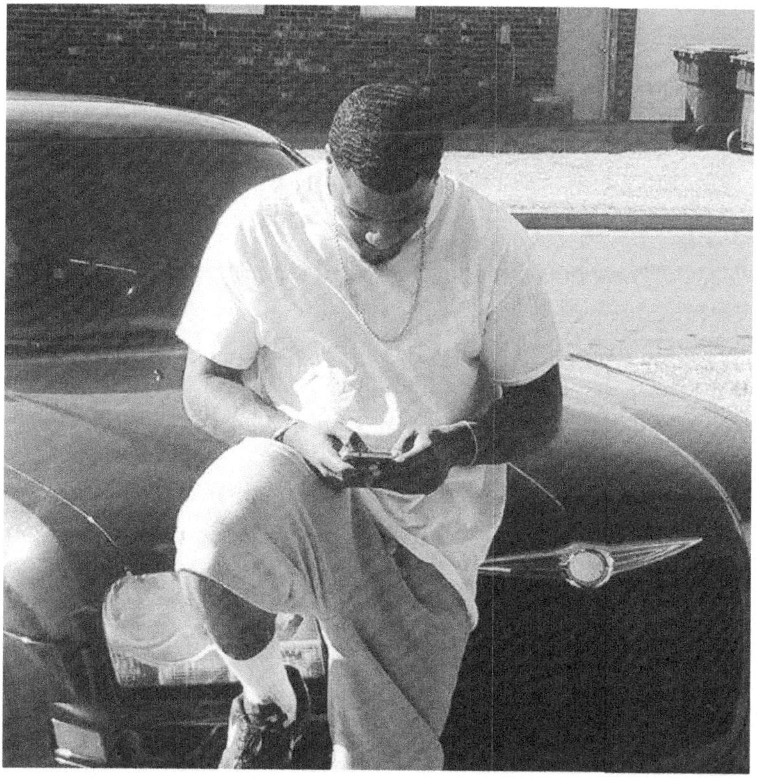

CHAPTER 11

"Naw don't reach," Edward said, opening the door. "Get the fuck out."

Pain looked at this lil bitty ass nigga holding a gun in his face. He turned his head and looked at his homeboy on the other side of the car. He looked at Big Rick. "I guess we gotta get out cuz," he said, smiling.

"Folks, I ain't got time for this shit," Big Rick said, getting out the car. "I'm fucking hungry."

"Mane how bout you shut the fuck up?" Edward said to Big Rick.

"What?" Big Rick asked. "Man fuck you." Edward gave Shorty a nod right before he kicked Big Rick in the leg. He fell to the ground hard. "Man, these Niggas ain't got no respect." He began rubbing his leg. Big Rick looked up and seen someone walking towards them. He smiled big once he realized who it was. He stood up and nodded to Pain.

"Yeah they must be Green people," Pain said as JK and Rachett walked up. "Bitches." Pain laughed.

"Fuck this," Edward said, cocking his gun. Before he could pull the trigger, JK put one in his dome as Rachett sliced shorty from ear to ear.

"Damn," Pain said as the bodies fell. "You Niggas right on time. What's the damn deal JK? Rachett Ro?" he asked, showing love. "What ya'll got up?"

"We was beating that ass on the table till you came in throwing bombs and shit like ya ass in Iraq," JK said, laughing. "Figured we stick around and make sure ya'll left breathing."

"Righteous my nigga," Big Rick said still holding his leg. "Wish you niggas would have stepped up before this short ass bitch kicked my fucking leg." Everybody laughed as Rachett Ro helped him in the back seat.

"So, what ya'll bout to get into?" Pain asked.

"Shit, head to Crime Bluff and get ready for this concert," Ro answered, closing the door. "Ya'll coming through?"

"Hell yeah we coming," Pain replied excitedly. "You now we not gonna miss Tutzilla and Reality."

"I can dig it," JK said, putting away his gun. "We out, see ya'll tonight."

"100," Pain said, getting in the car.

"Aight Rachett Ro." Ro nodded as Pain started the car.

"You good my nigga?" He asked Big Rick.

"Yeah man, I'm good. Nothing a good old hot bath won't handle. Let's move."

"Bet." Pain drove off headed towards the hotel. Once they made it and got settled in the room, he picked up the phone and tried to call Gripp, but he didn't get an answer. He called Kesha.

"What's up Bro?" Kesha asked when she answered.

"You good?"

"Yeah sis," Pain said responding. "I'm cool. Have you talked to Gripp?"

"Naw, but honestly, I haven't tried to call him, not trying to get cussed out today."

"Cussed out?" Pain said, smiling. "Who the fuck you shoot this time?"

"Now what makes you think I shot someone Pain? This time, it wasn't me."

"Oh yeah," Pain said, putting the phone on speaker so Big Rick could hear. "What the hell happened?"

"MaStarPeace shot Skanes in the leg and his bitch is in the basement."

"Who you telling my business to?" MaStarPeace said, walking in the room.

"This Pain girl," Kesha replied.

"Oh heyyyyyy future baby daddy," MaStarPeace yelled over Kesha. "You ready to give me that baby?"

"I see you still silly as hell," Pain said, laughing. "What's the deal with you MaStarPeace? It's been a minute. Sorry it's on these terms."

"Thanks Love," MaStarPeace said, taking the phone from Kesha. She got up and went in the living room with Yetta. "You just better be sure ya'll handle the asshole who killed my brother."

"Already on it, we bout to rest up for this show. Ya'll be careful and stop shooting people. That's our fucking job."

"Whatever, we good. Ya'll just be careful and see you soon."

"Already," Pain said as they hung up.

"How you doing sis?" MaStarPeace asked Yetta as she put the phone down.

"I honestly don't know girl," Yetta said, wiping tears away from her face. "I'm still waiting on my baby to walk through that door and hug me tight as ever."

"You and me both girl," MaStarPeace said as the tears started falling from her eyes. "Just like he did the night you almost killed Nick."

"Girl, that shit there was crazy as fuck," Yetta said, joking. "But that's also the night me and my girl Kesha got rid of what was bringing us down and found what we needed to bring us up."

"You ain't lying cause both ya'll was tripping that whole year dealing with the Nick and Tap show," MaStarPeace said, laughing. "You know it's bullshit when Tony and Pain didn't even know bout the Niggas or the shit they did to ya'll."

"Yeah, I know. Trust me Kesha does to," Yetta said as Kesha walked in the room.

"What you bitches talking 'bout in here that's so funny?" Kesha asked as she sat on the loveseat.

"We talking about you and Tap ass," MaStarPeace answered. They all laughed. "I was so glad when you stop letting that nigga ruin you. What had you so stuck to that nigga anyway?"

"Girl the head," Kesha said, smiling. "That nigga gave some bomb ass head. But he could never stop being a child."

"You stupid," Yetta said, interrupting her. "Too much information; don't wanna hear nothing about my brother cause I'm starting to see how he took you from that nigga Tap."

"Really, Yetta?" Kesha said, sitting up. "Tony didn't take me from Tap, he earned me. That brother of yours put in work from the first time he seen us at Walmart, when him and Yella came freshman year. I remember telling him I was on a mancation."

"What the hell is that?" MaStarPeace asked laughing.

"Umm," Kesha started. "That means I'm single, enjoying life and taking a break from men. At least until Tony's ass showed up." They all laughed in unison.

"Aight," Yetta said, getting up. "We been playing around long enough. It's time to go downstairs and see just what this bitch knows."

"OK," Kesha said as her and MaStarPeace got up from the couch. "Let's get it done."

They all went to the basement. Deanna was tied to a chair by the pool table. Yetta walked up to her and slowly took the tape off her mouth and said, "I hope you been down here long enough to have something important to say."

"The only thing I got to say is you bitches fucking up," Deanna said, looking at Kesha.

"I guess not," Kesha said. "Well I hope you're comfortable. Seems we gonna be here a while," Kesha said as she slapped Deanna. Blood came from her lip.

"Fuck," Deanna said, spitting on the floor.

Killa City
Killa City

TUTZILLA, REALITY, AND JUS_ROME

CHAPTER 12

"Man, it's lit in the town," Pain said as they were riding down Main Street. Janae, Karonda, and April were in the truck with them. Pain and Big Rick both dressed in Polo *KILLA CITY* t'shirt and the ladies were wearing nice, tight dresses with knee-high boots. "Its gonna be a hell of a night." He said rolling a blunt.

"You ain't lying," Janae said, passing Pain a lighter. "It's amazing how much the city showed up tonight. I see tags from all kind of states."

"Hell yeah," Big Rick said, pulling in the front of the old Looking Good as the Chevy Boyz turnt up the streets like a parade. "Pass me that bag ma."

"Here you go," Lanice said, handing him the bag. "You sharing that right?" She handed him a cup.

"You sure you can handle this D'usse?" Big Rick asked as he pulled out the bottle. "This ain't no wine cooler."

"Nigga please," Janae said taking the bottle. "You better act like you know. Better ask Tony bout me." She poured cups for everyone then they stepped out the car.

"Yo you see that Bentley across the street," Big Rick asked, pointing at the Royal Blue Bentley. "Somebody getting major money in Da Bluff."

"Ya'll see them tags?" Janae asked as she laughed and pointed at the army tags. "That's Marcus Woolfolk ride. Look like he got Doughboy with him. He got in town yesterday."

"Doughboy?" Pain asked. "You ain't talking bout my nigga Andre, are you?" Pain got up and walked across the street. "What up Campbell? What the hell you doing out?"

"Six Shooter Pain," Andre said, shaking his hand. "When you get in town?"

"We just pulled in bout thirty minutes ago," Pain said, looking at the car. "This shit popping."

"Hell yeah it is," Andre said, agreeing. "That's my guy Woolfolk. Woolfolk this the Prince of KILLA CITY, Pain Loc."

"What's good pimp," Woolfolk said, stepping out the car. "How you living?"

"Shit, obviously not good enough," Pain said, laughing. "I have got to get me one of these here. You mind?"

"Naw you good," Woolfolk said, stepping aside. "Any friend of Campbell's is a friend of mine."

"Righteous," Pain said as he looked around the car. "Damn this shit slapping, how much it hit for?" Woolfolk and Andre laughed. "What?" He asked confusedly.

"Bruh," Woolfolk began. "I don't even look at the numbers. I just walk in and drive away."

"Damn," Pain said. "Like that?"

"Like that," Andre said, nodding. They all looked up as the end of the car show was coming up. They could see Yung TutZilla and Reality sitting on top of a stretch escalade. "See how Crime Bluff shine?"

"Hell Yeah," Pain said, shaking hands. "We bout to get on down here to this Convention Center before parking get too tough."

"For real," Woolfolk said, opening his door. "Let's ride, Campbell." They both got in the car as Pain ran back across the street.

"Aye," Pain said as he got to the truck. "Time to ride ya'll."

"Bet," Big Rick said, unlocking the doors. They all got in and headed to the Convention Center. When Big Rick made the left off main, the streets were packed with people and cars. He seen a sign that said valet parking.

"Valet," Karonda said, laughing. "I bet that ain't cheap."

"Whatever," Pain said, pulling out money. "Go that way!" Big Rick turned into the hotel as Pain rolled down the window. "Aye," he said to the attendant. "How much is Valet?"

"It's $100. It's concert night," the attendant said. He walked to the window as Pain counted. "At least your vehicle will be close."

"I can dig it," Pain said handing him the money. "Here's two hundred, keep this truck close as possible."

"Yes sir," he said as he opened the back door for the ladies. Big Rick gave him another hundred. "Thanks."

"Already," Big Rick said. "Let's go."

They walked in the hotel and through the hall leading to the convention center. You could already hear Reality on stage hyping up the crowd. They got to VIP and took their seats just as Reality said, "NOW GIVE IT UP FOR ZILLAAAAAAA!" The crowd went crazy as the beat came from the speakers.

Gripp and Doe made it to Conway late. Doe picked up his phone to check the time. "Fuck, Gripp," Doe said putting his phone down. "I can't believe your slow driving ass made us miss the concert in Crime Bluff."

"Man knock it off," Gripp said, laughing. "You knew we wasn't going to the concert anyway. You hungry?" He rubbed his stomach.

"Shit," Doe answered. "I could eat. What you got a taste for? I could do waffle house."

"That's cool," Gripp said, turning left. "I need to call Bee." He pulled out his phone.

"Boss man, you might wanna hold off on that call," Doe said, pointing at the Wendy's parking lot. Doug D and Nine Milli were standing by the building.

"What the fuck they doing?" Gripp asked as they got closer. He knew that they couldn't be recognized in the rental, so he pulled in the parking lot and put the car in park.

"What you think Gripp?" Doe asked while grabbing two guns from the back seat. "We waiting?"

"Hell naw," Gripp said, grabbing one of the guns. "Let's go."

They both put on hoodies and got out the car. As they got closer, they could see someone sitting in the truck. Gripp's phone started vibrating. He looked and seen it was Kesha calling. "What's up Kesha?" Gripp asked when he answered the phone. "Now is not a really good time."

"You sure?" Kesha said, smiling. "I think you gonna wanna hear this."

"OK," Gripp said, motioning to Doe. "What?"

"Tomorrow, at eleven, it's a meeting in Little Rock that your guy Mr. Green is hosting. Supposed to be new investors and him announcing his new Distro. I don't know exactly where it is but I'm sure you will find out."

"That's some good information Kesha," Gripp said with a serious tone. "So, where did you get it?"

"We can talk about that part later Dad, I gotta go. Tony's coming," she said innocently as she hung up.

"What's up?" Doe asked looking at Gripp.

"I don't know, yet. Come on."

They both walked towards the truck. Doe came around the front while Gripp came from the back. It was only one person in the truck.

"Yo," Doe said, hitting the corner with gun in hand.

"What?" Nine Milli said, turning around. "Man put that shit away."

Gripp came from the back and said, "What the fuck you niggas doing?" He put his gun in his waist.

"Waiting on ya'll ass," Doug D said, lighting a blunt. "What the fuck took so long?"

"Cause Gripp drive slow as hell," Doe said, laughing. "But we were going to Crime Bluff. How the fuck ya'll waiting on us?"

"Cause Doe," Nine Milli began, "Your habits don't change. You gonna always find waffle house." They all laughed.

"Yeah whatever," Doe said, looking in the truck. "Who is that?"

"That's information. He is gonna tell Gripp something he wants to hear," Doug D said opening the door. "Ain't that right Troy?"

Troy got out the truck with his head down. When he looked up, Gripp noticed his eye.

"Damn," Gripp said. "What the fuck happened to him?"

"Oh, Troy here got knocked out by Doug D for putting a gun in his face," Nine Milli said, looking at Doug D.

"A lot of guns being pointed your way this week huh Doug D?" Gripp asked, laughing.

"It's nothing," Doug D said flexing. "I'll keep knocking niggas out. So, run ya mouth Troy."

"Well, tomorrow morning Green has a meeting at the Hilton on Broadway at eleven," Troy said, trying to scratch his head. "Every captain has orders to be there."

"Interesting," Gripp thought aloud, thinking about what Kesha said. "That's helpful news. Come on Doe!" Gripp walked towards the car. "Time to get some rest. We got a busy day tomorrow."

They both got in the car and drove off. Doug D got in the passenger seat. "Yo Nine," Doug D said. "You ready?"

BOOM BOOM!!!!!!

"YEP," he said, getting in the car. "We following them?"

Doug D looked at Nine Milli. "Why the fuck you kill the lil white boy?" He asked, pointing at Troy.

"That nigga work for Green," Nine Milli answered, putting down his gun. "I ain't taking no chances." He put the car in drive and sped off, catching up with Gripp and Doe. "Fuck him."

"What the fuck is going on down here? Tony asked as he walked into the basement. "Why the hell are you in my man cave at midnight, Kesha?"

"Nothing baby," Kesha said. "Glad that the lights were off, we just chilling."

"We?" he asked as he turned on the light. "Oh hell naw." He looked at the scene in front of him. "What the fuck ya'll do to Deanna?" Everyone stayed quiet. "MaStarPeace? Yetta? Kesha? Ain't nobody got shit to fucking say?"

"Look," MaStarPeace bravely said. "This bitch knew shit and we wanted to know. We didn't mean to kill her ass."

"We?" Tony asked, looking at MaStarPeace. "You mean you was in on this bullshit too?" He turned to look at Yetta. "Lil' sis, I told you we would handle this shit."

"Look baby," Kesha said, walking up to Tony. "I'm sorry."

"I don't wanna hear that shit," Tony said, yelling. "Now get ya'll asses upstairs so I can clean this shit up." He walked up to Deanna lying on the floor.

"Bruh?" Yetta asked.

"Now Yetta," Tony said, shaking his head as they walked up the stairs to the living room.

"He went off, huh?" Yetta said as they sat on the couch.

"Yeah he did," MaStarPeace said, pushing Kesha. "Somebody gonna get it tonight."

"I hope so," Kesha said, laughing. "I love it when he shows that power. Got my pussy all wet."

"Hell, mine too," MaStarPeace said. They all laughed.

The squad was up early and ready for the day. Everyone met at waffle house for breakfast. Gripp stepped outside and called Ma Williams.

"Good morning, Gripp," Ma Williams said when she answered. "How's your morning?"

"Hasn't started yet," Gripp responded. "I was wondering if you talked to the girls?"

"No not this morning; I'm really just getting up. We had a drive last night but finally made it."

"Where you drive to?"

"Oh, we're in Hot Springs. This is where the Baker Brothers are hiding, so we gonna go have a chat."

"Fuck yeah, we going after Green at his big meeting today."

"Now how you expect to get in that meeting?"

"I'm gonna walk right the fuck in and mingle."

"You truly are a crazy King; I know you will handle this accordingly."

"Yes ma'am," Gripp concluded, hanging up the phone.

Gripp went back into the restaurant and ate with the fellas. After they were done, they loaded up and hit the slab. He pulled out his phone and texted Pain to let him know he was on the way. He turned up the music and sat back as they rode to the Rock.

They made it to Little Rock at 10:40. Doe pulled into the car wash where Pain and Big Rick were waiting. Gripp checked his surroundings before getting out the truck.

"What up Pain?" Gripp greeted, walking up. "Ya'll ready to end this shit?"

"Fuck yeah," Pain answered, rubbing his neck. "Got me up early and shit. Ya'll heard about what happened last night?"

"Last night? Naw we got in late and went straight to the hotel. I thought you were at the concert last night?"

"I was," Pain said, opening the trunk. "That's when the shit popped off."

"Wait," Nine Milli said, interjecting. "*CRIME BLUFF* is neutral grounds, who the fuck is that stupid knowing the consequences?"

"Man, I don't know," Pain said, passing out guns. "But someone got hit and they looking."

"Hell yeah they looking," Big Rick stated, stepping out of the car, and grabbing a gun. "Real OG'S ready to blast. Shit I seen Mickey and Bennie riding the East side then on the way out I seen Rome, Luis, and Boolou on the North. Somebody better talk fast."

"Aye," Gripp started, closing the trunk. "Two things; one, if it does pop off, *KILLA CITY DEFENDS CRIME BLUFF* ya dig? Two, watch ya backs and let's handle this shit and go home whole." Everyone nodded. Gripp turned and started walking towards the hotel. He closed his eyes for a second to get in his mode.

"Yo Doe, is it that time?"

Doe looked at his watch and replied, "Yeah, BREED."

Gripp pushed through the door as the crew followed behind him. No one exposed their guns as they went to the elevator. Doug D hit the button and the elevator doors opened immediately. They stepped in and headed towards the top floor.

Green was having a meeting with his captains. He looked around and seen that everyone was there but Nick. He looked at Smooth Da Dude.

"Where in the fuck is Nick?" He asked with a mad look on his face. "He is supposed to have Gripp's body by now!"

"Nick's taking care of what Nick need to take care of," Smooth said, standing up. "I'm his right hand and you need to come on with this bullshit ass meeting so we can get the fuck out of here."

"Why is it you have such a smart mouth like you don't work for me?" Green asked, lighting a cigar. "You and your captain both need some home training."

"Home training?" Smooth asked, walking towards the desk. "I'll show you..." JP stopped him before he got all the way disrespectful.

"Naw Smooth," JP said, patting his shoulder. "This ain't the place."

Smooth nodded and they both went to sit back down.

"Now that we got dumb shit out the way, it's time for a new mission since, obviously, the crew I told to do it can't get it done. After this meeting all of you, along with my son's Big Ben and Hassan, will go to KILLA CITY and kill Gripp's whole crew."

"What," Jimmy interjected. He laughed as he continued, "So you want us to go against a kingdom with your ignorant sons leading us? Shidddd we may as well kill ourselves."

"Shut the Fuck Up," Big Ben said loudly. "I'm tired of y'all and the disrespect. Nobody eats till that nigga dead. Laugh bout that." He turned and walked out the room. Green got up and grabbed his glass.

"Let's go have some fun," Green said. They all walked out of the office and into the ballroom to wait for the other guests. They sat on the couches and poured drinks. Green opened the safe under the bar. "Alright, everyone knows what to do."

One by one they all put their guns inside the safe. Green chose this hotel for its class and security so that his guests would know he could handle their money. When they were done, Green closed and locked the safe.

"Our guest should arrive here shortly so relax and enjoy until then," Green said, turning to sit on the couch. He looked up when he heard the elevator bell sound.

"Well I guess they're early. Aaron, go show them in."

"Yes sir," Aaron said getting up and walking to the main elevator. When he turned the corner, his eyes got big as he looked into the eyes of the King of *KILLA CITY*. He tried to scream, "Gre..," but Gripp grabbed him and choked him out. He let his body fall to the floor.

"Yo Nine," Gripp said, popping his knuckles. "Throw that nigga in the elevator. Use his head as a door stop."

Nine smiled as he swung the body into the elevator. When he turned around his smile was gone. He said, *It's game time,* to himself.

Doe started walking into the meeting hall. Doug D was right behind him. He could hear talking coming from another room, so he headed in that direction. He peeped around the corner then turned back to the squad.

"It's 'bout 4 to 5 niggas in there and I think I see that bitch Green," Doe whispered.

"What about Nick?" Nine Milli asked.

"Let's find out," Doe answered as he stood up and walked into the room. He cocked his gun. "What's good bitches," he said as he fired off a shot, almost hitting Big Ben.

"What the fuck?" Green yelled as *KILLA CITY* walked into his meeting. "How the fuck did you get in here?"

Smooth flipped over the coffee table and drinks went everywhere. He grabbed the gun he had in his ankle and fired shots, making everyone take cover.

"JP, come on!" he screamed as he pulled his shirt. They both ran to the service elevator and jumped in. As the doors were closing, Big Ben was running towards them with Doug D shooting behind him.

"Fuck," Big Ben said as the bullet went through his arm. He dove into the elevator as the doors closed. Doug D shot a few more times at the elevator door before he went back in the other room.

"Couple of them niggas got on the elevator, Nine Milli, let's go!" Doug D yelled. They both stepped over three of Green's captains before they got to the elevator. Nine Milli hit the button then turned to look at Green who was still sitting on the couch.

"Bet ya bitch ass wondering how much longer you gonna be breathing huh?? Nine Milli asked him. "Well before you go, I should tell you today's life lesson."

"And what's that you sloppy son of a bitch?" Green asked, attempting to stand up until Doe push him back on the couch.

"Sit down little guy," Doe commanded, looking at Green and his whole squad bloody. "This is important information my nigga telling you so all ya'll watch and listen."

"WATCH?" Green confusedly said. "Watch what?" Doe turned Greens head towards Nine Milli. He gave a nod and Gripp came around the corner lighting a cigar.

"SUP Bitch," Gripp said, smiling, and showing off his grill. "Am I late for your meeting?" He walked closer as Green started shaking nervously. Gripp sat on the other side of the couch. He looked at Green and laughed hard.

"I know this nigga didn't just shit his fucking pants," Doe said, stepping back, and laughing. "You scary nasty fucker. And this is who you niggas follow? Bitches." Doe said as he shot two of the three captains left in the room.

"Aye Nine Milli," Gripp said, getting up and walking to the window. "Go ahead and tell him the lesson." Gripp opened the patio doors. "Nice view."

"DON'T FUCK WITH *KILLA CITY*," Nine demanded as him and Doug D got on the elevator. Doug D kicked the body out the way so the doors would close.

"Doe, bring that bitch over here," Gripp ordered as he turned and went back to view downtown Little Rock. "You see Green," Gripp continued as Doe pushed Green on the patio. "What I don't understand is what the fuck made you think you could come for the King and live to tell about it?" He hit his cigar.

"Fuck *KILLA CITY*," Green said, knowing he was about to die. "You going down one way or another."

"Oh, you must mean FeFe? That's being taken care of as well. And you right," Gripp said smiling and throwing his cigar over the patio. "I am going down except I'm gonna use the elevator. Now go get my cigar."

"What?" Green asked as Gripp spun and picked him up by the neck lifting him like paper. He threw him over the patio and watched as his body hit the ground hard.

"Let's ride Doe," Gripp commanded, walking back to the elevator. "You hungry?"

"Hell yeah, but what we gonna do bout this nigga?" Doe asked, pointing at Jodi still lying on the floor with a bullet in his leg.

"The last man standing, huh? Fuck it. Kill that bitch too."

Doe walked over and shot Jodi in the head then went back to the elevator. He reloaded as they descended to the bottom floor. When they made it and stepped off the elevator, everyone looked as they walked to the exit of the hotel.

Doe noticed a man pulling out his phone. "Y'all crazy as hell, Im calling the police," the man said before Coye slapped his phone out his hand.

"What are you stupid?" Coye asked the man, looking at him crazy. "That's the King of *KILLA CITY* and he will kill you and the dumb ass cops."

Doe smiled, walked up to the young kid, and asked, "What's ya name lil man?"

"Coye Tippy from *Crime Bluff*," he answered, putting base in his voice.

"RIGHTEOUS," Doe said, handing Coye a wad of money. They walked out and got in the truck with Doug D and Nine Milli. Doe looked at the time. It was 12:16. "Hell yeah, we might make it home in time for the Cowboys and Eagles' game."

"Oh, we gonna make it," Doug D said. "I'm behind the wheel and I got bread on the game. Gotta watch my boys get in them birds' ass."

"My niggas," Gripp said, laughing. He texted Ma Williams to let her know Green was done before he sat back and enjoyed the ride. They headed back to *KILLA CITY.*

CHAPTER 13

"Baby," Kesha said, walking into the bedroom. "you awake?" She looked at Tony sleeping. "You sexy big dick ass nigga." She pulled the cover revealing his naked body. She grabbed his dick and slowly took it in her mouth; letting her tongue touch every part that she could fit.

She heard Tony moan as she sped up, giving him that amazing feeling, but teasing him at the same time. She stopped. She used her teeth, gently biting and playing with the head.

"Damn baby," Tony said as he opened his eyes. "Shit."

He put his hand on her head and closed his eyes, knowing the skills that her mouth had. He felt it and she did to. She pulled her head back and jerked his dick hard as he shot cum all over them both.

"Now that's how you wake a nigga up," Tony said, looking at Kesha.

"You know I don't like you mad at me baby," she said, getting a towel. "But Bam is dead and I want answers. We really didn't mean to kill her ass."

"Who killed her?" Tony asked, but Kesha didn't respond. "What, cat got your tongue?

"No," she replied, laughing. "I hear you, but it doesn't matter, she's dead and that's it."

"Well ok," Tony said, rolling out of the bed. "What time is it?"

"It's 5:19," she said, rubbing his face. "You been sleep for a while."

"Them damn pills Dr. McFadden gave me," Tony said, throwing the pill bottle. "Knocked my ass out! Where's Yetta and MaStarPeace?"

"Yetta is cooking cheese dip for the game and MaStarPeace is working on her eulogy. Gripp and the guys should be here soon."

"Oh yeah, did they get them Bitches?"

"Well Gripp killed Green and we haven't heard from Yella on FeFe."

"What about Nick and the Baker Brothers. They still walking?"

"For now, now go shower and get dressed. It's almost game time."

"Already," he said, going in the bathroom. "I'll be down in few."

"OK," she said, walking out the room.

"Oh, what the fuck!" Tim yelled as the Cowboys scored another touchdown. "How the fuck these Cowbitches keep fucking scoring?"

"What you mean how?" Marcus asked, laughing. "Cause the Eagles suck!"

"Mane, what the fuck ever!" Tim said, pulling out his phone. "I'm bout to hit this nigga Nick 'bout our bread."

"Why?" Marcus asked, taking a shot. "Gripp ain't dead."

"But Green is," Tim stated. "And that's his bank. I'm not gonna keep going at this nigga unless I know my money coming."

"Did Green son pay that bill for having us kill Bam?" Marcus asked.

"Yeah he paid after talking shit cause it was Bam and not Tony but it was too late by the time we knew who it was," Tim said as he dialed Nick.

"What the fuck you want nigga?" Nick answered with an attitude.

"What's your fucking problem?" Tim asked, looking at his phone. "You know who the fuck you talking to?"

"Naw, nigga do you?" Nick asked. "Why the fuck did you stupid niggas kill Bam? That's not what the fuck I paid you to do. That's not the order I gave!"

"Well shit changed," Tim responded. "And money talks. I don't give a fuck; the nigga dead, it's part of the game."

As he was talking to Nick, Marcus looked at the game. Neither one of them seen Half Ton and Blake come into the bar. They sat at the table a few feet from them and watched as the game went to overtime.

"DAMN IT," Tim yelled. "Fucking overtime? I'm going to take a piss." He got up and went to the bathroom. When he came out, the bar was empty. "What the fuck?" He said, reaching for his gun. "Fuck, left it in the car." He walked towards the bar and stopped when he seen Marcus with Blake's gun pointed at the back of his head.

"Get your ass over there," Half Ton said to Tim. Tim looked at him before he started walking. "Have a fucking seat."

Tim sat down beside Marcus as Ma Williams walked into the bar. Tim and Marcus both sat up straight.

"Hello Brothers," Ma Williams greeted. "Hate to meet on such bad terms."

"Look Ma Williams," Marcus immediately said. "It was a contract. You know we don't choose sides."

"Contract?" She said. "There was no contract for the senseless killing of Bam. Why would you lie to my face Marcus?"

"Ma Williams," Marcus pleaded. "If you talk to the Boss she will explain."

Tim hit Marcus in the back and shouted, "Shut the fuck up!"

Ma Williams pulled out her phone and dialed Shirley's number. She answered on the second ring.

"Ma Williams," she saluted. "To what do I owe this call?"

"Hello Shirley," Ma Williams greeted. "I'm here with your brothers and I'm about to take their lives for killing Bam. Marcus here seems to think you have a way to save them."

"Ma Williams, you know the rules," Shirley began. "If we take a contract, we take it. As far as responsibility, that's on the person who paid the contract."

"So, there was a contract on Bam?" Ma Williams asked. "Who paid it?"

Shirley thought for a second and replied, "If I give you the names you have to let my brothers live. That's the deal."

"Done," Ma Williams said. "Now, who?"

"Big Ben paid $750,000 for Tony's head. They didn't know it wasn't Tony till it was too late. Nick pulled out on the hit once he found out Bam was killed."

"Tony?" she wondered. "If my son was dead, we wouldn't even be having this conversation, but I will keep my word and let your brothers live." She hung up.

"So, what's the word Ma Williams?" Blake asked.

"Half Ton," she said. "I want you to beat these muthafuckas until your hands get tired and then Blake, I want you to continue. I promised to let them live, not walk." She turned and walked out the bar as Half Ton met her demands. Blake looked up at the game.

"Oh shit," he said happily. "Cowboys won."

Ma Williams got in the truck and dialed Gripp's number while they finished inside the bar.

"What's good Ma Williams?" Gripp greeted when he answered.

"King," she responded. "I'm here with the brothers. Turns out Big Ben put a hit out on my son. Tell me you killed him already."

"Naw, that was one of the assholes who made it to that service elevator so he in the wind."

"Damn, I made a deal for that information to let the Baker Brothers live."

"I hope you gonna at least fuck they ass up."

"Oh, Half Ton and Blake are having fun in there. We will be back tomorrow before the wake begins. Have we heard anything on FeFe?"

"I talk to Yella about an hour ago, she got on a plane to Canada. I told him to come on back, so he won't miss the funeral chasing her ass."

"Alright, see you tomorrow," Ma Williams said as she hung up the phone.

The next morning, Kesha was sitting out by the pool enjoying the morning breeze as MaStarPeace came outside.

"Good morning," MaStarPeace said, sitting down. "What you doing?"

"Girl nothing," Kesha answered, hiding her iPad. "Just letting my mind wander. How are you? Did you finish your eulogy?"

"I'm here," MaStarPeace said, reaching for the iPad. "Should be done in a few. What's this you working on?"

"It's a poem MaStarPeace," Kesha said, reaching for her iPad. "Now give it back."

"Naw," MaStarPeace said, laughing. "Let me read it."

"You get on my nerves," Kesha said, laughing. "Go ahead."

MaStarPeace read the poem and felt the tears coming out of her eyes. She could feel the love in every word Kesha wrote about her brother.

"Damn Kesha," MaStarPeace said, wiping her face. "This is really good. I didn't even know you still wrote poetry."

"I write when I have something I wanna say, and I needed to get that out. I'm missing my bruh."

"Me too girl, me too. Well this gives me an idea for tonight."

"What's that?" Kesha asked, sitting up.

"We should all go to Ice Event Center tonight. I know a few people performing."

"I'll ask but you know Gripp ain't really into that type of thing."

"He will like this; *Belle Poetry* is hosting, and *Poetic City* is performing. It will be a good show."

"OK, I will ask at breakfast."

"Thanks girl, come on we gotta get to Gripp's before they eat all the food."

They were the last ones to make it to Gripp's. Tony got out and opened the doors for the ladies. They all went inside. They made their way to the dining room were everyone was waiting.

"Well it's about time," Yella said grabbing his plate. "We was about to eat without y'all."

"Yeah," Kesha said. "Right." She laughed as Tony held her chair.

The table was quiet. All you could hear was chewing. MaStarPeace kicked Kesha's leg. She looked up and rolled her eyes.

"So, everyone I have an announcement," Kesha said, getting everyone's attention. "Tonight, after the wake, we all are going to Ice Event Center to relax and unwind before we bury our brother tomorrow."

"Ice?" Doug D said. "On the Eastside?"

"Yeah," Kesha said, looking at Gripp. "And we going, right?"

Gripp looked at her, then at Yetta, and then back to Kesha. "Yeah, we going," he said before he went back to his plate.

After they finished breakfast, Kesha and MaStarPeace went to work on the slide show. Ma Williams and Yetta prepared food for the wake. Tony, Yella, and Doug D detailed Bam's 300 while Nine Milli rolled blunts.

"Looks like everyone is trying to stay busy," Bee stated, coming in the bedroom. "How are you Gripp?"

"I'm numb baby," he answered. "I never expected to have to bury any of these guys. It's just gonna be a hell of a weekend."

"Well we will get through it like we always do," Bee said, kissing his cheek. "Now get ready. It's almost time to go to the funeral home."

It took a few hours for everyone to get dressed and ready to go. All the men were sitting downstairs waiting for the women to come down. As usual, they were taking forever. Gripp heard his alarm beep so he turned to look at the camera. He could see Richard and Alex pulling up in the driveway.

"Alright Squad," Gripp said, grabbing his coat. "It's time to move. He walked to the stairs. "HURRY YA'LL ASS UP!"

Tony opened the door, and everyone started going outside.

He said, "I see we did a hell of a job," while looking at Bam's 300, shining like it was fresh off the lot. He reached in his pocket and pulled out the keys. When he hit the start button, the speakers instantly started bumping Yung TutZilla.

"That was Bam's shit," Kesha said, coming out of the house. "HOTTEST IN THE CITY."

"My nigga," Yella said, looking at the ground. "Let's get this shit over with." He pushed through everyone and got in his Charger.

"That nigga tripping," Gripp said, laughing. "Load up. I know people already showing up." Everyone moved. Gripp and Bee got in the limo with Ma Williams and Faba. Tony drove Bam's 300 with Kesha, Yetta, and MaStarPeace while Richard and Alex followed behind. Nine Milli and Doug D both rode their bikes. Half Ton and Blake rode with Janae and April who came back with them the night before.

The limo pulled out and everyone followed. When they made it to the end of the driveway, Detective White was there to escort them to the wake. He waved as the cars started passing by.

"Fucking Asshole," Tony said as they passed Detective White. Kesha hit him on the arm.

When they pulled up to Vance Funeral Service the parking lot was already full. "Damn," Kesha said, looking at the lot full of cars. "Don't they know this is just the wake?"

"Bam just touched that many people," MaStarPeace said. "On top of being in *KILLA CITY* so the streets gonna show love."

And love they showed. When Yetta and Kesha walked in the building, they could see the pictures and flowers that the city had made and put out for Bam. Yetta instantly started crying. It was a beautiful sight to see.

"Mane they got it set up like the president died," Gripp said as they took their seats.

"Naw," Ma Williams said. "Trump wouldn't get half this respect."

As everyone came in and out, speaking and hugging, the night was calm. Pastor Fuller stood by the casket raising his hand to get everyone's attention.

"Praise the Lord Saints," Pastor Fuller said as everyone repeated. "Even though this is a heartbreaking occasion we're going to praise God, because we know He's got Bam. Now, I know some of you are tired and need a nap, but, after the wake tonight, the family will be attending the Ice Event Center for some 'relaxation' as sister Kesha called it. We're going to have a song by a very dear friend of the family after which we will dismiss. Now everyone please show some praise for our sister Ms. Ashley Williams.

"Thank you," Ashley said as everyone clapped. "Well I was going to sing a gospel song tonight, but my girl, Yetta, requested something else, so I hope you all love it. The instrumental to Puff Daddy's *I'll Be Missing You* came on. “Tony, help me out,” She said as the whole room started grooving with her. The angel started singing her tears out.

As they finished the whole room cried and cheered at the same time.

“Ya’ll know what it is,” Tony said. “Everybody be safe tonight and come out and join us as we celebrate our brother.” He looked at Yetta then at MaStarPeace. He hugged Ashley then grabbed Kesha by the hand as they led the way out of the funeral home. Everyone headed out and got in their rides as Tony let the doors up on the Chrysler.

“Did you call Proverb and let him know we were coming thru tonight?” Kesha asked MaStarPeace.

“I sent him a text message when we left the house,” MaStarPeace answered, putting on her seatbelt. “He said the red carpet is out.”

“Red carpet, huh?” Kesha said smiling.

Killa City
Killa City
Killa City

CHAPTER 14

It took about twenty minutes to get to Ice. Once again, the parking lot was full, and you could smell the food as soon as you got out your ride. As promised, the host did roll out the red carpet. He came out to greet everyone.

"Wassup, family!" Proverb said, speaking to Tony. "I'm glad everyone could make it out tonight. Yetta," he said, hugging her. "I'm so sorry for your loss."

"Thank you," she said, hugging him tight. "And thank you for putting this together so fast."

"No problem," Proverb said as he turned to the right. "King, it's an honor," he said, shaking Gripp's hand. "I have a section ready for all of you and we have an awesome show tonight."

"Thanks, fam," Gripp said.

"Come on in. It's time to start the show," they demanded as they all followed him into the building. He showed them all to their seats once they walked in.

"Hey, are the ladies from *Belle Poetry* performing tonight?" MaStarPeace asked.

"This is their show," Proverb answered. "Auntie is hosting it with me and Jus_Courtney is around here somewhere."

"OK," MaStarPeace said, looking around. "I will try to catch them later."

"Cool," Proverb said. "Y'all enjoy the show."

Proverb walked off as Doe and Yella went to get drinks. They came back just as the waiter was taking food orders. After the waiter left you could hear the music start and Auntie get on stage.

"Hey, hey," she said, dancing on stage. "How's everyone doing tonight. Good? If you good make some noise." The crowd responded with screams. "Man, we packed in this place tonight." She looked around in the room. "That means I better not leave here with any books which are on sale here by the stage." Everybody laughed and cheered. "Normally we don't do this on a Friday night, but tonight is different. Tonight, we have the King of *KILLA CITY* and the whole squad here to bid farewell to Bam cute ass. Sorry, Yetta," she said as they all laughed together.

"You always starting mess," Proverb said, joining her on stage. "Y'all give it up for Auntie." Even Gripp stood, clapping for Auntie. She smiled and took a selfie with Proverb before he continued. "We got some great artists performing tonight," Proverb continued. "So please sit back, have a drink. We even got some of the best food in town being cooked right back there." He pointed towards the kitchen. "And the bathrooms are clean."

The crowd laughed as the music played. Proverb and Auntie walked throughout the room, taking pictures, and greeting people. After several minutes, Proverb got back on the mic.

"Alright now, the first poet I'm gonna bring to the stage is one of *Poetic City* finest, the syl in syllabus, give it up for Tavie The Poet!"

Everyone stood to their feet as Tavie hit the stage in his Saints *Poetic City* hoodie. "What's good?" Tavie said as he grabbed the mic. "Hope ya'll alright tonight."

"How bout dem Cowboy's?" Tony yelled from the table. Everybody laughed

"I see Tony already going in about that lucky win," Tavie said, pulling out his phone. "I'm gonna Cash App you that hundred right now though," he said laughing.

"That guy there," Tony said, laughing.

"Aight since I see we have some Kings in the building," Tavie said. "I'm gonna do a poem called *KING SHIT*. What's up Gripp." The lights went low. When he rose his head, they came back on:

Plotting my next move on you niggas
Shuffling commas into a deck of six figures
Blue faces knocking at my door
Trapping in the bag of my eyes but no time to be tired

Gunning down the pussy
Ducking and dodging her mental
Ain't got no love for her feelings
This connection keeps losing signal

If I ain't feasting like a King

Then I ain't solve the riddle
Gave up wishing upon the stars, nuclear I'm the reaction
Some Niggas grind ain't up to par

How you stacking money just to stay in the streets
Lost desire for the fame and street names
Rather wear a suit staring out large window frames

"Elevating on you niggas
Show you how a King supposed to lead!"
KILLA CITY: TAVIE THE POET.

Everyone stood to their feet and gave a reaction that rang through the building. Gripp got up and walked to the stage. "*King Shit*," he said, smiling as he shook Tavie's hand. He turned and went back to the table and applauded with the rest of the crowd.

"Thank you," Tavie said. "RIP BAM." He left the stage and went to the kitchen. Auntie came back on the mic.

"Hey," she said from their table. "Belle Publishing still got books over here, but, in the meantime, ya'll vibe to the music while we take a short break."

The DJ played music as everyone moved around the room. The waitress came to the table with the food. She handed them to Doe as he passed the plates around the table. Mac Woods stopped by the table and shook hands with everyone.

"King," he said, shaking Gripp's hand. "Nice of you to come out tonight. Sorry for the loss of your soldier."

"Appreciate it Mac," Gripp said, looking at Richard and Alex. "Excuse me for a second." He got up and walked to the back of the table. "What the fuck ya'll doing?"

"This *TV the Poet* keeping trying to get through," Richard said, holding him back. "Says he wants to speak to MaStarPeace."

"MaStarPeace," Gripp said, signaling her to come over.

Tavie said, "Tell ya Ques to relax."

"It's ok," MaStarPeace said, touching Richard on the arm. "He's cool. How you doing, Tavie?"

"I'm good," Tavie said, hugging MaStarPeace. "Sorry about your brother. I know how close you guys were."

"Thank you Tavie, we really appreciate it."

"Already," Tavie said looking around. "I gotta go find a seat. Mac about to perform. I'll see you later."

"Ok," MaStarPeace said, going back to her seat as Proverb came back on the mic.

"Aight y'all ready for the next poet?" Proverb asked, loving the crowds reaction. "Give it up for the black Shakespeare himself, my guy, Mac Woods!"

Mac bounced on to the stage as *Shook* by Mob Deep played through the speakers. He grabbed the mic:

Ducked taped, soaking from his own blood...
"YOU KNOW WHO YOU FUCKIN' WITH?"
Stuffed in his trunk with a gun in his face and that's all he could come up with.
BAM! BAM! BAM! Left my gun smoking...

SON, THEY SHOOK! Scared to death, scared to look...
SON, THEY SHOOK!
Cause ain't no such things AS HALFWAY CROOKS!
When the crowd repeated the hook, Mac went in.

Money, power, respect; ingrained since a toddler.
Rimmed passions, distrust majored, crack houses was my neighbors.
Genesis of a lost innocence; eyes accustomed to drug deals gone mean.
Drive byes daily, babies sleepin in their cribs become victim.
My big cousin went out like Caine's cousin
Trying to catch his breath in the street, burgundy painting his white tee.
No CPR cause its too late...dapping coke transactions on ghetto landscapes.
Learned how to move in a room full of vultures.
These niggas loud but don't pop shit...a room full of holsters.
Now heavy in the game with a bad queen on my side...

Keisha'll suck the chrome off a Chevy then shoot up ya Momma's Camry.
A video vixen sprawled all on these Range Rover seats;
Persian rug guts, a tech nine laying between her legs while rolling my weed.
Blue-black, sexy muthafucka lookin' like a moonlit masterpiece.
Private affairs, we roll with a tighter crew...
Bout 20 hood ass nigga's in designer suits.
Mansa Musa ruling with an iron fist.
War against the kingdom...bet ya whole re-up the sire wins.

SON, THEY SHOOK!...Scared to death, scared to look...
SON, THEY SHOOK!
Cause ain't no such things AS HALFWAY CROOKS!

Flashback to when the nigga first tried me...
Shootout in Oakcliff, near 15th; his shit jammed but mine released.
I blew his brains out in the winter breeze.
Later that week, brought his momma a bouquet and kissed her on her cheek.
This my jurisdiction...niggas better try it never...
Came in this world alone but I'll see that these bitch niggas leave together.
What you know about buying a gun, shaving the numbers off...
Dippin' half a brick in detergent just to throw the dogs off?

Life's a bitch and Ima long dick her to get paid.
We came up traveling hard but down the wrong way...
And niggas do anything for attention.
Be careful, the streets are good to make examples
Swear you want smoke but mice in a jungle only get candles.
Big Mama kept me in church...God, forgive me for I'm losing faith.
From my closest friends sent to you in thunderstorms of shell case.
More Kody than MLK.
Momma just gone have to forgive the hood for the monster it made.
THIS *KILLA CITY*, NIGGA!...was born a switch hitter; just adapted to the pain.
KILLA CITY: MAC WOODS

The crowd went crazy as Mac jammed on stage as the beat walked him off. He walked by the table and Gripp grabbed his hand. "It Ain't no such thing as Half-Way Crook," he said, smiling. "I like that shit. Yeah, I fucks wit it." He sat back down.

"Hell Yeah," Doe said. "Cause I was born a switch hitter Mac. Knock 'em out with either fists." They all had a good laugh at Doe crazy ass. "Naw but that was some good shit Pimp."

"Yo," Mac said humbly. "I'm glad y'all dig it. Bam was a good guy so I had to do it one time for *Killa City*."

"Respect," Tony said as Auntie got back on the mic.

"Y'all enjoying the show so far?" Auntie asked, loving the crowds' reaction. "Well, you know I'm gonna say that we still got books over here by the stage. You need to grab one before I tell King Gripp." The whole crowd laughed at Auntie, including Gripp. She continued, "Ya'll give it up for *Killa City*."

The crowd applauded. "We lost a great friend, a brother, and a son when we lost Bam. May he rest, knowing the joy he brought and left behind in this world."

"YOU BETTER SPEAK AUNTIE!" Shay and Carlos yelled from the back of the room.

"But it did bring someone home," Auntie said. "Hit it DJ." *Boo'ed Up* by Ella Mae began playing from the speakers. As the lyrics came on, the crowd vibed.

"FEELINGS, SO DEEP IN MY FEELINGS. NO, THIS AIN'T LIKE ME. CAN'T CONTROL MY ANXIETY."

The crowd was singing along when Auntie came back on, "Yeah, she not gonna perform but she will do a walk on this stage with them cute Dawgs. Ya'll stand to ya feet and give it up for that girl that says she ain't Boo'd up, she Que'd up. Come on up here MaStarPeace."

Yella laughed, "I told you Auntie always calling people out. Watch Kesha, you gonna be next." Everyone at the table laughed.

"Auntie better leave me alone," Kesha said, laughing as MaStarPeace stood on stage with Richard and

Alex behind her. The crowd was singing her remix B*a-dum Que'd up, buddy Ba-dum Que'd up."*

By the time MaStarPeace finally got back to the table, her food was cold. "See this is what you get playing with Auntie," she said, holding the cold fish. By the time she finished her sentence, Proverb was already putting another plate in front of her.

"Aye," Proverb said. "We got you." He walked off to get back to the show. "Alright ya'll ready for some more entertainment?" The crowd clapped.

"Alright," Auntie said, going on stage. "We gonna take a short break cause the ladies are gonna close out the night. I wanna thank *Killa City* for buying up our books."

The crowd applauded as she hugged Bee. "Relax and mingle," she continued. "Cause, I still got one more trick up my sleeve." She smiled as she walked off the stage.

"I'm glad we came out tonight," Gripp said, putting his arm around Kesha. "I gotta admit it is relaxing."

"I told you," Kesha said smiling. "You ready for tomorrow?"

"Hell Naw, but it is what it is."

"Kesha," MaStarPeace said, touching her arm. "So, you gonna do that poem you were working on?"

"Girl," Kesha said, shaking her head. "I ain't getting on no stage. That was a lifetime ago."

"So, it's like riding a bike. Tell her Yetta."

"It is a good poem," Yetta said, nudging Kesha. "Why not?"

"Cause, I don't want to," Kesha answered, rolling her eyes. "Now shut up about it."

MaStarPeace looked at Yetta. Yetta got up and said, "I'll be back. Going to get a drink." She walked off and went to the bar and stood beside Proverb.

"You enjoying the show Yetta?" he asked, signaling the bartender over.

"Yes," Yetta said. "You outdid yourself on this one."

"It's not hard when you always surrounded by talent, the show basically outdid itself."

"You just bring the best out of people," Yetta said, hugging him. "Which is why I need you to do something for me."

"What's that?"

"Get Kesha on stage," Yetta said pointing. "She needs the release."

"Kesha?" Proverb said confusedly. "She hasn't been on stage since freshman year. She been writing?"

"I don't know how much but she definitely has something for tonight. You just gotta work your magic." Yetta said patting his back.

"I got you," he said, paying for their drinks. "Let me go holla at Auntie."

Proverb left as Yetta walked back to the table. She sat back down and gave MaStarPeace a wink. They both sat back as Proverb came back on the mic.

“Alright, now we gonna change it up and bring out a sexy voice to listen to. This next Poet can write about anything. And I do mean anything. So, I want ya’ll to show some love for my girl SHARITA RENEE!”

Sharita came on the stage, looking like a sexy apple in a red *Backs to My Roots* dress with knee high boots. She stepped on the stage and grabbed the mic as the whole room got quiet:

This poem is called GO FUND ME
He called me out of breath
Said he was running from 12
And it’s gonna be around 12 I’m like what the hell
It just never fails
Bruh I can’t keep getting you out of jail
No, I won’t keep posting bail
I can’t keep being up at night wondering if you are alright or worse, have these cops killed you this time.
I’m not ready to see your face on a t-shirt
Having females coming out the woodwork
Saying you was giving them that woodwork
See cause when your gone, that’s when people wanna ride your wave
Put flowers on your grave
But throw dirt on your name
Don’t be surprised how people change
A hard head makes a soft ass
Stop running these streets like you get a lifetime pass

How much longer will it last
Oh, until somebody cut you down
So, what's going on now
Hello!
I said what's going on, today?
Because I don't have a place for you to lay
Hello!
Hello!
Hello!
There was no reply
A few hours later, knocks at my door
When I seen the red and blue lights
I fell to the floor
He called me out of breath
I'm fussing not knowing that was his last breath
Another GO FUND ME page to be made
SharitaRenee *KILLA CITY*

Sharita's words moved the crowd. As she finished, everyone was on their feet, applauding. She walked off stage with a big smile on her face as she hugged Bee. Pain stood, hugged Sharita, and said, "That hit me hard girl, how did you know?"

"I didn't, but thank you," she said and went to her seat as Auntie came on the mic.

"Now what you think about that huh?" Auntie asked the crowd, holding her arms towards Sharita. "Amazing. The night is almost about to come to an end, but before it does, we have one more poet. Now she hasn't been on stage in a while so be easy on her. Stand to your feet for Gripp's Princess, Ms. Kesha G."

Kesha looked at Auntie like she just lost her mind.

"Which one of ya'll did this," Kesha asked, looking at MaStarPeace and Yetta. Neither one of them said a word as Kesha stood up. "Your ass is mine," she whispered before walking to the stage and taking the mic from Auntie. After they hugged, Auntie walked off stage.

"Well isn't this a surprise?" Kesha asked, smiling and thinking about how she loved being on the stage. "I didn't know I was part of the show. We all know we can't say no to Auntie though." Everybody laughed. "I actually do have something I wanna read for you all." She pulled out her phone. When she looked up, Gripp and Tony were both standing by the stage waiting for her words. "This poem is called *BLACK BUTTERFLY*:

Love conquers all
But what combats love for the streets
A desire to survive
At any cost
To live free
Shit
To eat
My family matters to me
The next man will risk his life for his
These streets don't love us

It don't give a damn if we spread our wings
Couldn't care less if we lived
Pitted against one another
In a psychological prison
Warfare and welfare
No justice
But my J's are clean
These streets don't love us
It don't give a damn if we spread our wings
Couldn't care less if we lived
Stuck in caterpillar form
Afraid to break free
Every day, we hustlin'
For dollars
For a dream
For direction out the hood
Would we really escape
If we could
There's no honor amongst thieves
But there's a code to these streets
One of mine for one of yours
That's just the way it goes
When will this shit get old
How long will it take to see
These streets don't love us
It don't give a damn if we spread our wings
Couldn't care less if we lived
But this black butterfly

She lives
She lives because of her Kings
Her hedge of protection
Guardians of her well being
They honor her as a future Queen
Realizing her worth
Blocking all possible pressure
Keeping away danger sight unseen
These streets may not love me
Or give a damn if I spread my wings
But my Kings
They protect me from a harsh reality
They allow this black butterfly
To be free
To escape
Never again will I be a caterpillar stuck and afraid
This black butterfly will spread her wings
and achieve any and everything

Once Kesha looked up, there wasn't a person sitting. The entire room was on their feet for Gripp's Princess.

"Now that's how you end a show," Auntie said, walking back on stage. "Thank ya'll for coming out and please be safe getting home. You ain't gotta go home but you getting the hell outta here." She exited the stage as the crowd began to leave.

"Yo, everybody get home and rest up," Gripp commanded, standing up. "Tomorrow gonna be a long day."

They all nodded as they got up from the table. Doe stood behind Gripp and Bee. Tony took Kesha's hand and led her and Yetta outside while Richard and Alex walked with MaStarPeace.

"What's up Doe?" Gripp asked, looking behind him. "Everything good?"

"Oh, everything Gucci," Doe answered. "I'll go home after I make sure ya'll get home. And it ain't no request ya dig?"

"Yeah," Gripp said, walking towards the door. They stepped outside as everyone departed ways respectfully. Gripp closed the door to the limo and they left Ice, headed home.

The next morning Kesha woke up early. She went downstairs and made some coffee. Her mind was moving in so many directions. "Good morning," she greeted Yetta as she came down the stairs. "How did you sleep?"

"High," Yetta replied, laughing. "I took a sleeping pill. I haven't really slept since Bam died."

"I know sis, one day at a time," Kesha said while hugging her.

"I know, my brother still asleep?"

"I'm about to go wake him up now, gotta find an outfit for today. And make sure you shine for Bam," Kesha said, grabbing an extra coffee mug for Tony.

Yetta smiled as Kesha walked back up the stairs. She sat the cups on the nightstand then reached over and touched Tony on his face. He rolled over.

"Good morning beautiful, how are you?" Tony asked as he kissed her hand.

"I'm here daddy, I'm here. I made you some coffee."

"Thanks baby," he said, sitting up. "What time is it?"

"7:40," she replied, looking at her phone. "I'm gonna find something to wear. You should shower."

"Yes ma'am," he said as he went in the bathroom. "I'll be out in a few."

YELLA

CHAPTER 15

Yella and Doug D pulled up to the pool hall. They walked inside and met up with Pain and Half Ton. Everyone was already dressed and ready for the funeral.

"It's already starting to look like the movie Colors," Half Ton stated, looking at everyone's attire.

"Well you know Bam would've wanted it that way," Pain said, dusting off his Dickies. "Gang banged out cuz."

"Hell yeah," Yella said, grabbing his keys. "Y'all bout ready to head that way? It's almost that time."

"Yeah it is," Gripp said, looking at Kesha. "Let's do this." He reached and grabbed Bee's hand as he led the way. Everyone followed behind as the limousines were pulling into the driveway. Gripp and Bee got in with Ma Williams, Faba, and Blake.

Kesha rode in the other limousine with Yetta and MaStarPeace while Tony drove the Three Hundred with Richard and Alex. Yella rode on the passenger side. Half Ton, Nine Milli, Doug D, and Doe led the pack on motorcycles.

It seemed like a long ride to the church where the funeral was being held. It also seemed as if every bump they hit took joy from everyone.

"I don't know if I can go through with this," Yetta said as they were getting closer to the church. "I never thought I would see this day."

"None of us did," Kesha interjected, handing her a tissue. "But it's here. At least Bam would be proud of our wardrobe," She said, laughing. They were all dressed in red and black. "What's up MaStarPeace, you good?"

"I'm here," she said, folding a piece of paper in her hand. "Just getting my mind right."

"Well, I hope it's right cause we here," Kesha said as they pulled into the parking lot of the church. The parking lot was already full, with most of the people from Bam's wake.

"It's a lot of people in town for the funeral I see," Yetta said as they drove through the crowd. She waved at Dr. McFadden as they passed.

Doe stopped his bike in front of the door then turned and looked at Nine Milli. He nodded and they both started spinning tires and doing donuts in front of the church. When they stopped, *Killa City* came through the smoke, and walking up the steps. Gripp turned and smiled as he opened the door and propped it open.

"Now I like that entrance," Gripp said, laughing. He watched as Tony grabbed Ma Williams and Bee out of the car and escorted them up the stairs. Yella went and got Kesha and Doug D got Yetta. After they were all inside the church, Gripp went back down and met with Mr. Vance while Richard and Alex helped MaStarPeace inside the church.

"It should be some seats left on the front row," Tony said as MaStarPeace walked by. "I'm gonna wait on

Gripp." He turned his attention back to Gripp as the Ques went in.

"Yo Vance," Gripp said handing him $20,000. "Nice job with my man's. He looks straight with that outfit on."

"Well," Mr Vance said, putting the money in his pocket. "Ma Williams said she wanted it simple. I figured Jordan jump suit with matching shoes fit Bam."

"You ain't lying. That's what he would've wanted," Gripp said. Pulling a box out of his pocket, he continued, "Do me a favor though and put this on Bam before we start."

Mr. Vance opened the box and said, "Wow!" He looked at a *Killa City* chain made of black diamonds. "I will go do this now." He shook Gripp's hand and went into the church.

"You ready?" Gripp said, turning and looking at Tony.

"Yeah Boss," Tony said, moving the block from in front of the door. "I'm ready."

They all walked in a line with Gripp and Tony leading. Doe, Pain, Doug D, Skanes, and Nine Milli followed. As they walked down the aisle, they saw a lot of old friends.

"I see the old hood showed up," Tony said, pointing at Tego and Blow. "Must have had a carpool."

Gripp also noticed Yung TutZilla and Reality were in attendance as well. When they were almost to their seats,

Pain turned and waved at Poetic City who took up a whole section of the church. Everyone finally made it to their seats as Pastor Fuller came to the pulpit.

He spoke with a mild tone as the choir hummed, "PRAISE THE LORD SAINTS! TODAY WE ARE TO LIE TO REST SOMEONE WHO TOUCHED LIVES. HE WAS A HUMBLE SOUL AND WILL TRULY BE MISSED BY HIS FAMILY, FRIENDS, AND LOVED ONES".

♫*I'M COMING UP ON THE ROUGH SIDE OF THE MOUNTAIN AND I'M DOING MY BEST TO MAKE IT IN*♫

Pastor Fuller continued, "NOW I KNOW YA'LL USED TO THOSE LONG DRAWN OUT FUNERALS WHERE EVERYBODY GET UP AND WANNA TALK ALL DAY, BUT NOT TODAY. THE FAMILY HAS A PROGRAM CONSISTING OF A SOLO BY ASHLEY WILLIAMS, *THE EULOGY* BY MaStarPeace, VIEWING OF OUR LOVED ONE, THEN WE'RE GOING TO THE CEMETERY AFTER WHICH THE FAMILY WILL HAVE FOOD AND DRINKS AT THE ICE EVENT CENTER."

The crowd clapped as the pastor signaled Ashley to the stage. As she stepped to the pulpit, she greeted the audience, "Hello everyone. My name is Ashley Williams and I will be singing *Take My Hand Precious Lord* by Mahalia Jackson."

Ashley's voice reminded everyone of Whitney Houston. The crowd was in tears. Pastor Fuller came back on stage as Ashley handed him the mic and said, "Y'all. Ya'll give it up for Ashley and that beautiful voice." The crowd clapped as she took her seat. "That's why we don't need a longer service. I know Bam would not have wanted all these tears. Now we will have the *Eulogy* by Bam's sister, MaStarPeace."

MaStarPeace walked on stage as the choir hummed *Amazing Grace*. She laid her paper on the pulpit and looked at the crowd.

Killa City
Killa City

May You Find Rest

This silence has become a stillness that's
impossible to move.
This emptiness inhabits a vessel that's impossible
to fill.
This grief is inconsolable,
I mourn for you.
For myself as well.
I mourn in your absence that I have yet to accept is
reality, because you were just here laughing,
smiling, living.
It is to dust and ashes that you must return,
It is your laughter and your spirit that we yearn
for.
I wasn't prepared for it to happen so soon,
To have to go through life without you.
Nightmares don't only occur when we're asleep,
but I have yet to awaken from this slumber that's
held me hostage to my grief.

My dear brother, now six feet deep beneath the circle of life that has now run its course and requested rest.
May you find rest where the Sun never extinguishes
May you find rest where pain can never disturb your peace and sadness is a myth.
May you find rest where you don't have to worry about fear.
May you find rest with the Most High, my dear brother.
As your flesh begins to deteriorate into small ant hills, I promise not to let anyone trample on your name, tarnish your legacy, or discredit your contributions as I fight to preserve those hills because they are all I have left of you.
Now, I understand why smiles are so memorable,
While laughter is shared universally, it's shared especially special with certain people.
I miss laughing with you.
How your voice coming through the other end of the phone was the only pick me up I ever needed,
How your presence was my shield of protection that yielded me from the world's cruelty.

How your love was always enough to pull me back together.
Forever engraved in my heart,
I will cherish the time that God allowed me to have with you regardless how brief.
I will reflect and conjure up our memories,
I will keep your name alive and carry it everywhere with me.
I no longer need to mourn your absence because I know that you will always be with me,
My guardian angel got his halo and wings,
My guardian angel found his eternal peace.
All I ever wanted was for you to get home safely,
To your heavenly residence that's been patiently awaiting your arrival.
My dear brother,
May you find peace.
May you be at it,
as well.

After she finished, the room was speechless. She looked at everyone's eyes, walking off the stage, and kissing Bam's casket as she went back to her seat.

Pastor Fuller walked up, grabbed the mic, and said "Well now wasn't that a sermon we needed to hear? AMEN!"

The audience shouted, "AMEN."

Pastor Fuller continued, "I know I did. Now we will view our loved one after which we will head out towards the cemetery. Choir," He said pointing to the choir. They began to sing *Amazing Grace* as rows started moving to see Bam. They all shook hands with the family after viewing.

"Yo," Tutzilla said to Gripp when he made it to him. "Really sorry for the loss homie. Why didn't you call me?"

"Because you would've told me not to retaliate," Gripp answered, showing his homie love. "Thanks for driving down though."

"Already, it ain't no thang. I'll see you at the cemetery."

"Bet," Gripp said, noticing it was their time to view Bam. "Tony, You, Kesha, and Yetta go ahead."

"Aight," Tony said, grabbing Kesha and Yetta by their hands. "Ya'll ready?"

Neither one of them spoke a word as they walked up to the casket. Once they got in front of him, Kesha slid her hand away from Tony's and leaned on Bam. She seemed to whisper something in his ear before kissing him on the cheek. Her tears fell to his shirt as Tony pulled her back so Yetta could have her time.

"I miss you baby," Yetta said as she looked at the man who was her whole world, lying there. "At least you look good Daddy." She kissed his lips then fixed his shirt before turning and walking out of the church, holding Kesha's hand. MaStarPeace ran after them.

Gripp tried but Ma Williams held him back. "Let's finish," she said to Gripp. "We can deal with that on the way to the cemetery. They alright." Ma Williams turned and walked towards the casket as everyone followed. No one wanted to see Bam in that way, so no one really took a long time.

"What up nigga," Pain said as he put a ring on Bam's finger. "Can't believe this shit is real. Hundred my nigga. We got ya seed." Pain walked off as he saw Tony walking up.

"Yo," Tony greeted. "We gonna take off so we can stop by the store and grab Kesha a BC. We'll meet ya'll at the cemetery."

"OK," Pain said, shaking his hand. "Be safe nigga."

"Already," Tony said, leaving out of the church. "Ya'll ready?" He asked the ladies.

"Yeah," Yetta said, getting in the car. "I'm so ready."

"Did you look at Bam?" Kesha asked MaStarPeace.

"I don't need to see him," MaStarPeace said. "I know he is still with me." She got in the car while Big Rick and Blake walked up, waving.

"What's up fam?" Tony asked when they made it to them.

"Green son in town," Blake said, looking around. "At least that's the word."

"Oh yeah," Tony said. "We just gotta get today out of the way. He's tomorrow's problem."

"Aight," Blake said, closing the door for Tony. "We behind ya'll." He left and they got in the truck with Richard and Alex. They all left the church.

Tony pulled over at 7-11 and Richard pulled into the liquor store next door. As Tony got out and opened the doors for the ladies, a van pulled up beside him. He held the door open as Kesha, MaStarPeace, and Yetta walked in.

While Tony was at the register, he seen Big Ben walk in, but didn't recognize him. Big Ben walked around the store following Kesha to the register.

She went and stood beside Tony as MaStarPeace set her Red Bull on the counter. Tony looked up at the door and seen Jake, Billy, and Smooth who he knew worked for Nick. He instantly tried to reach for his gun, but Big Ben grabbed his hand.

"No no no Tony," Big Ben said, holding his arm. "We not gonna do that. Take 'em." He commanded to his crew.

They all grabbed MaStarPeace and Kesha, dragging them out of the store while everyone just stood there dumbfounded. Kesha screamed but didn't see anyone come from the liquor store.

Yetta grabbed a wine bottle and hit Billy in the back of his head. He fell instantly. She jumped on Smooth's back and tried to choke him, but he wrapped her up and ran outside. Smooth threw them in the van and tied them up as Tony and Big Ben were coming out.

Big Ben put a silencer on his gun then turned and shot Tony in the leg. Kesha tried to fight her way out of the van, but Smooth punched her in the face and closed the door when she fell.

Big Ben grabbed Tony's phone and dialed Gripp's number. Gripp was getting in the limo when his phone rang.

"What up Tony?" Gripp said when he answered. "What you need?"

"You killed my dad," Big Ben angrily said. "And now you will pay. I have your daughter and you have seventy-two hours to deliver ten million to me or I will kill her."

"What the fuck," Gripp said, looking at the phone, knowing who was on the other end. "You got who? I know you didn't make the mistake of putting your hands on my daughter?" Gripp signaled the crew over. "You dead nigga."

"See, I had a feeling you wouldn't believe me," Big Ben said as he cocked his gun. Skanes pulled in on the bike shooting as Big Ben aimed his gun and shot twice. He looked up and seen men running towards him. He jumped in the van and rode out as Skanes slid the bike into 7-11.

"DAMN," Blake said. "Not again. Call Gripp!" He said, falling on Skanes. "Breathe my nigga." Blake held his wound. "Get the fucking truck!" Richard ran to get the truck while Big Rick called Gripp.

"Yeah," Gripp said while out of breath. "Where the fuck ya'll at?"

"We at the 7-Eleven right off the highway," Big Rick said. "Bitches shot Tony and Skanes. And took Kesha, Yetta, and MaStarPeace!"

"Let's go, now!" Gripp yelled, jumping in the driver's seat! Everyone jumped in the limo as Gripp smashed out of the parking lot.

Reality looked at Tutzilla and asked, "What the fuck going on bruh?"

"I don't know fam," Tutzilla replied, grabbing his keys. "Come on." They hopped in his escalade and sped off behind Gripp. Everyone was standing outside of the church clueless when Ma Williams walked out with Faba and Yella.

"Why ya'll looking like that," Yella asked a group of people. "Where's the squad?" Yella walked in front of Ma Williams and looked around but didn't see anyone. He turned and looked at Faba. "What the fuck?"

Faba pulled out his phone and noticed he had a missed called from Arkansas. He showed the number to Ma Williams. "Nick," Ma Williams said, reaching for the phone. "Give it to me." She took the phone and dialed the number. He answered fast.

"Yo Faba," Nick said when he answered. "They coming for ya'll."

"This is Ma Williams, who is coming for us?"

"Ma Williams," Nick said with respect. "It's Big Ben and a few others. The niggas came to my crib with this plan to kidnap Kesha and Yetta for ransom and you know how I am about Yetta so I tried to dead it, but my people can be real stupid."

Ma Williams interjected, "So why help *KILLA CITY* now? You just tried to kill Gripp."

"I took orders because that's what we do; I'm good with running my little city. Green just chose me and you don't tell Green no."

"Stay close!" Ma Williams said, hanging up. "Yella, call Gripp."

"Yes ma'am," Yella said, pulling out his phone. Here you go."

Gripp felt his phone ring as they pulled into the parking lot. He jumped out of the car, ignoring the call as he ran to the body on the ground.

"SON-OF-A-BITCH!" Gripp yelled through the parking lot. "FUCK!"

"He's still breathing," Blake said, holding down the pressure on Tony. "Let's get him in the truck."

Blake and Doug D picked Tony up and set him in the back on the truck. "Doug D and Skanes," Gripp said. "Take Tony to the hospital! Let no one touch him but Dr. McFadden!"

"Bet!" Doug D said as they got in the truck with Tony and Blake.

"Man, fuck this," Doe said, pulling out his phone. "It's time to put an end to these pussy ass niggas."

"Who you calling?" Pain asked as he ran up. "I know this pussy didn't take my sister."

"Yeah he did!" Doe said, putting the phone to his ear. "They shot Tony, plus he got Yetta and MaStarPeace! I'm killing this nigga whole blood line."

"What up?" Black said when he answered. "How you living?"

"Bad Bro! Sunset Village," Doe said.

"What? Who?"

"Big Ben! He got Gripp and Ma Williams' daughters. He got MaStarPeace too."

Black looked at the phone, said, "I'm on my way," and hung up.

Gripp walked over with fire in his eyes. He turned and got in the limo as Doe got in the passenger seat. They pulled off. "Nigga got my baby, Doe," Gripp said, speeding towards his loft.

Pain felt his phone vibrate. Ma Williams and Faba pulled in with Yella.

"What?" he said when he answered the phone.

"Yo," Tim said. "We just seen them bring in Tony. I'm telling you now that wasn't us."

"Yeah, I know. It was Big Ben bitch ass and he got my sister."

"Anything you need." Tim said in a serious tone.

"One hundred," Pain said, hanging up. "Let's get the fuck out of here." Pain walked off and got in the car with Ma Williams. "They shot Tony; it's bad. And they took the girls."

"What does he want?" Ma Williams asked.

"I don't know," Pain answered. "But he won't live to have it." Ma Williams' phone rang. She looked down and her eyes got big. She showed the phone to Pain.

"Oh shit!" Pain shook his head. "You gonna answer?"

"Hello," Ma Williams said when she answered. "What is it?"

"Problems, Rosie," Cain Loc said. "Problems. And I'm hearing you got a lot of 'em."

"It's nothing I can't handle," Ma Williams replied. "How did you hear so fast on the yard anyway?"

"Because it's my business to know," Cain Loc said. "I'm sending Quick and Quick Duece. Find them girls and end this shit before I do." He hung up.

Ma looked at Pain as he asked,

"What he say?"

"Biggs coming; put every crew in every city on this. five million for the heads of the people who took our girls." She tossed the phone to Faba.

EXCERPT FROM KILLA CITY III.

THE FINAL CHAPTER…

Faba looked at Pain then back at her. "Aight," Faba said while dialing a number.

"Yeah," Nick said when he answered. "What's up?"

"Your people got Yetta," Faba said. "Where the fuck they going?"

"Them bitch ass niggas went against my word?" Nick screamed through the phone. "Mutha fuckas!" Nick hung up the phone and dialed Smooth but didn't get an answer. He took a chance and called Yetta's phone.

"Seriously," Big Ben said when he answered. "What the fuck you calling this phone for?"

"Nigga I told you not to make that dumb ass move, that's why you will forever be a corner boy."

"Dumb, huh? Them bitches gonna either pay up or I will kill all three of these bitches one by one."

"Three? I know your dumb ass don't think the King of *KILLA CITY* gonna pay you and let you live after taking his daughter on the day of Bam's funeral. All you idiots are walking dead men."

"Naw Nick, we untouchable," Big Ben concluded as he hung up.

Nick looked at the phone to see how long they talked. He dialed Wallace's number.

"Rayford Bail Bonds," Wallace said when he answered.

"Yo, I need a trace. I'm gonna text you the number," Nick said.

"Aight Boss," Wallace said, opening his computer. "How soon do you need this info?"

"ASAP!" Nick replied as he hung up. He texted the number then went to change clothes. He came out, grabbed his keys, and left the room.

"I can't believe these hoe ass niggas!" Nick got in the car still talking to himself, "Put his hands on my girl. I gotta get her back." He hit the garage button and put the car in drive. He pulled off until he seen people standing in front of his car.

"What the fuck?" Nick heard the "CLICK CLACK," from a gun that one of the men were holding.

"Get the fuck out the car," Doe said as he and Gripp came into the light. "Stand up for the King."

"FUCK," Nick said opening the door.

Made in the USA
Coppell, TX
26 June 2026

83158000R00105